LANGELY EASED HIS REVOLVER FROM THE
HOLSTER AND STEPPED IN FRONT OF THE
OPEN DOORWAY. . . .

"Not tonight."

His words riveted the men, and the whiskey bottle
slipped from Lowe's fingers. Langely stepped into the
light and shot a quick glance at Sidney Lowe. "Try for
it."

Lowe's hand stopped and carefully backed away from
the revolver on his hip.

"Thank God!" Lemont exclaimed.

Langely motioned with his revolver. "You boys stand
over there, away from the desk. Marc, relieve your visitors of their hardware."

"With pleasure," Lemont said, standing.

At once Langely realized his error. He read it instantly in Lowe's eyes, and in that brief moment when
Lemont's body moved between them, Lowe's gun appeared in his hand and fired. . . .

Dell Books also by Douglas Hirt

ABLE GATE
A PASSAGE OF SEASONS
DEVIL'S WIND

The
Silent Gun

Douglas Hirt

A Dell Book

Published by
Dell Publishing
a division of
Bantam Doubleday Dell Publishing Group, Inc.
1540 Broadway
New York, New York 10036

ISBN: 0-440-21311-8

Printed in the United States of America

Published simultaneously in Canada

May 1993

10 9 8 7 6 5 4 3 2 1

RAD

For Dave, Arlene, Matthew, & Jacob

1

Atop a dusty ridge where the sere grass burned copper in the late-afternoon sun, Thomas Langely reined his horse to a stop and sleeved a muddy streak across his forehead. In the valley below, a glistening ribbon of beaten silver nudged against the flanks of a town where buildings mingled with the cottonwood and the willows that grew near the water.

He returned the hat to his head, recalling the town up north he'd left behind. It was the trees and water, he decided, that made him think of Miles City, Montana. Both scarce commodities in this parched land called the New Mexico Territory. But there the similarities ended. Miles City was a checkerboard boomtown of crisscrossing avenues, tall buildings, wagon-clogged streets, and two thousand bustling people.

This place, on the other hand, didn't appear to be booming anywhere! It was an odd blend of wooden one-

and two-story structures and squat adobe hovels. A broad main street divided a dozen or so false-front buildings squeezed in awkwardly among the more gently flowing lines of the adobes—curious structures to the eye of a northerner.

Narrow alleyways quartered the town, and at the north end a wide wooden bridge spanned the shallow river. East of the bridge was the livery—smaller than the Ringer and Johnson Livery, which he'd left behind only a month earlier. Strings of corrals stretched out behind the livery, and a nervous wind pump chattered as it sucked river water into a wooden cistern.

Langely arched his back, feeling tight muscles give reluctantly. The horse twitched beneath him, and he reached out a hand to stroke its strong, smooth neck, wondering if he should give this town a try. He glanced at the sun, low on the horizon. It wouldn't do any harm to spend the night. In the morning he could decide.

Langely started the horse down the ridge, then remembered something and drew up. He unbuckled the gun belt and in the harsh evening light studied the worn Colt revolver. With a frown he folded the belt around the holster and tucked it into his saddlebags. If he intended to leave his past behind, he was going to have to leave it all. The gun was his last tangible tie with a life that had become too desperate to live. In a year, in a month, or maybe a week, the feel of a gun on his hip would be forgotten; he'd get used to it—he'd have to.

The hollow clip-clop of steel-shoed hooves against timbers brought him across the bridge at the north end of town. A row of low adobes stood off to his right, the livery to his left. Farther up the street he reined to a stop in front of a grand two-story structure with gold-

and-silver letters scrolled above the second-floor balcony.

THE SILVER LADY SALOON.

On the balcony two ladies whom Langely suspected would be more likened to a color of a different hue than *silver*, talked carelessly at the railing. They became aware of him watching, and one of the women said something that made the other laugh. She leaned over the railing and winked, then covered her face coyly with a paper fan with which she had been waving away the stifling New Mexico heat and retreated into the darkness of an open doorway.

Langely grinned and turned an eye along the dusty street. A barber shop–bathhouse stood opposite the saloon. North of it rose a large stone bank building. South, a narrow, false-fronted adobe with the words ESTEROS CREEK GAZETTE painted in green on a shingle.

He nudged his horse forward in the easy manner of a man accustomed to saddle life, passed an adobe eatery and a clapboard general store. A narrow alleyway ran down to the river. Across the alley was the sheriff's office. The town continued on in the shape of unidentifiable adobes and tinder-dry wooden shops, trailing out eventually to more red dust.

The Montgomery Hotel across from the sheriff's office reminded him vaguely of the Olive Hotel as he angled his horse toward it.

Without warning, a black carriage turned a corner and cut across his path, its bright yellow-spoked wheels throwing up a spray of dust. His horse reared back and spun away. At the reins an old man glanced up from beneath the brim of a wide hat and heaved back at the pair of matched chestnuts.

"Sorry, mister," the old-timer said as the carriage rolled past. "Didn't see you coming up."

Langely calmed his horse and took appreciative note of the girl sitting next to the old man. Her dark eyes flashed critically at him from above the high cheekbones. Her smooth skin was the color of bronze, and a long, thick braid of black hair trailed down her straight back from beneath the frilly brim of a white sunbonnet. She wore a blue dress with ruffles around the high neck, and short sleeves puffed up at the shoulders.

She studied him briefly but thoroughly in that moment when their eyes met, and Langely knew she was reading the signs—the crusty growth of a beard, the dusty corduroy vest that had seen too many nights in a bedroll—signs that spoke of a man who comes and goes as the spirit moves him, a man best avoided.

Then she turned away and adjusted the bonnet upon her head. Langely nosed his horse into the rail in front of the Montgomery Hotel and dismounted. Through the curve of his saddle he watched the carriage move up the street and disappear around a corner. *A mighty fancy rig for this part of the country,* he thought, dismissing the incident. He untied the saddlebags and slid his Winchester from its scabbard.

The hot air inside the hotel bore the musty weight of stale cigar smoke and creosote. He dropped the rifle and saddlebags on the desk and slapped the bell.

A tattered sofa atop a threadbare carpet faced the plate-glass windows. Along the back wall a staircase climbed to a dimly lit hallway. A tall floor clock stood silently alongside the stairs, its pendulum motionless; time suspended at quarter past three. Langely checked the Elgin watch in his pocket. Six o'clock, and the oppressive desert heat was still nearly too much for a man used to more northern ranges to endure.

He rang the bell again.

"Yes, yes, can I help you?" the man said, coming in from a back door, brushing chicken feathers from the sleeve of his black coat. He squeezed behind the desk and smiled widely, wiping his hands upon his pants. He was a jovial fellow, with a bright, full face, red cheeks, and a bald head that seemed too pale to belong to someone from New Mexico. He widened green eyes that rolled around as if not firmly fixed in their sockets.

"A room," Langely said, and wrote a name in the register that still flowed awkwardly beneath the pen.

The clerk pressed a blotter to the fresh ink. "Will you be staying with us very long, Mr. Bracken?"

Bracken. Thomas Bracken. The name had a foreign ring to it. One more item that would take some time getting used to. . . .

"A few days, maybe longer."

"Business? Oh, I don't mean to be inquisitive, it's just that we have so few visitors come to Esteros Creek." His face flushed.

"Perhaps. If I find a nice, friendly place, I might settle down for a while," he said truthfully.

Green eyes widened even more. "Well, Mr. Bracken, Esteros Creek is a nice little town, a good place to raise a family—do you have a family?"

"No."

"We're a growing town," the desk clerk tried again. "There's even talk of the railroad coming through in a couple years. Lemont at the *Gazette* says the Santa Fe already has rails laid through Raton Pass, up north. In a few years . . . ?" He shrugged his shoulders hopefully.

"What do you do, Mr. Bracken, if you don't mind me askin'?"

Thomas Langely looked at the white-hot glare of the afternoon sun coming through the dusty windows, beating the once jade-green sofa to a sort of neutral gray color. "I'm a storekeeper," he lied. "Had a hardware store back in Illinois. Sold out last winter and started drifting. Maybe I'll open another someplace." He looked back.

"An honorable occupation, Mr. Bracken, bein' a storekeeper. A growing town needs good solid citizens like shopkeepers and bakers and barbers and—er . . . er, the like. You are going to like Esteros Creek, a good town for a store, a nice, quiet town—" He broke off his sales pitch and his head jerked toward the door.

Langely's hand jumped reflexively. He stopped himself at once and glanced at the desk clerk, but the little man had not noticed the movement. He was squeezing out from behind the counter and heading for the open door. The gunfire that had erupted down the street was quickly blooming into what sounded like a little war being fought at the edge of town.

Langely wiped a damp palm on his vest and shoved his right hand into his pocket, following the little man to the door.

Riders galloped into town from the south, dust boiling up beneath their horses. They charged past Strathmore's Undertaking Parlor, cavalry fashion, whooping and yelling, and churned the street into powder as they pounded by the hotel. The staccato bark of their guns blasted holes in the hot, blue afternoon sky. Startled horses pulled at their hitching rails as the riders swept into town like a desert dust devil. They reined to a stop in front of the saloon, where the cloud of dust caught up with them, overtook them, and settled back to the road as fine red powder.

Some of the riders burst through the batwing doors, while others stayed outside, beating the red chalk off their clothing and scattering out among the other shops.

"A nice quiet town?" Langely said, pulling back inside the hotel.

The clerk grinned and shook his head. "Don't pay them no mind," he said, squeezing back behind a counter too close to the wall to accommodate his rotund dimensions gracefully. "Them's the boys from the Double T. You can expect 'em every Friday about this time—regular as a clock. . . ."

He paused, glanced at the back wall, and gave a chuckle. "Well, regular as most clocks. They come to town to raise a little Kane and spend their money—good for business, you know. Come Sunday morning they'll all be heading back to work, dead broke and toting a hangover this big!"

"And what do the local authorities think of their shooting up the town?"

"Burt Jenney? He don't mind much. He punched cows himself once, a long time ago. He knows them boys's just blowing off a little steam. He doesn't say much as long as nobody gets hurt—usually no one does."

"Usually?" Langely hitched up an eyebrow.

"You know how men are." He grinned. "Sometimes they get drunk and . . . well." He leaned close, as if there were anyone near to overhear. "Even old ladies and wild goats start looking good to 'em." He laughed, and poked Langely in the shoulder. "But that don't happen often. Nope, the only time Burt starts to real worrying is when hands from the Double T and them from the Largo happen to be in town on the same day, sort of like mixing matches and dynamite, if you know what I mean."

Langely knew all too well. Miles City, Montana, seemed a place far removed from this hot land of New Mexico, but people were basically the same wherever you went, and that is what concerned him.

"Here's your key, Mr. Bracken. Room Two-oh-one. Overlooks the street."

"My horse is out front."

"Got a boy will take him over to the livery for a nickel."

Langely dropped a coin on the desk and carried his belongings up the creaking stairs.

2

Room 201 was a blast furnace, and like the rest of the hotel it reeked of old tobacco smoke. Thomas Langely dropped his rifle and saddlebags on the bed and threw up the window, but no breeze moved the thin curtains. Low, red rays cut through dusty desert air as the setting sun resisted the coming night, fighting to retain its death grip upon the oven-baked land.

He leaned out to study the street below. Opposite his window stood the sheriff's office, its doors and windows flung wide to vent the summer heat. The large building across the alley from the sheriff's office was a general store—JOSHUA LAWRENCE, PROPRIETOR, carefully lettered on a shingle. Farther up the street, shoehorned between two larger buildings, squatted a low adobe with a name painted across the front in faded red. LA CASA LUNA. Even the language here was different.

The saloon was doing a thriving business. A line of

horses tied to the hitching rails stretched down the street, and a steady flow of men parted her swinging doors.

He vaguely wondered where all these men came from in so isolated a place as Esteros Creek. His view came back and halted on the fancy carriage that had nearly run him over. It was now tied in front of the general store. He thought of the girl with the haunting black eyes, searched a moment for her unsuccessfully, and pulled back into the stifling room.

A lean, gray-headed man in a long black coat had an elbow pressed into a small stack of newspapers at the hotel desk as Langely came down the stairs. He was speaking with quick, animated gestures, stabbing the air with a stub of a cigar locked between his fingers when the squeak of a stair tread brought his head about.

"Mr. Bracken!" the desk clerk said, motioning him over. He turned his enthusiasm on the man standing there. "Mr. Lemont, this is Mr. Bracken. He's the shopkeeper from back east I was telling you about." When Langely came over, the clerk said, "Mr. Bracken, this here is the owner and editor of the *Esteros Creek Gazette,* Mr. Marcus Lemont."

"And might I add," Lemont said with a smile, "the *Gazette*'s only employee. Nice to meet you, Mr. Bracken." He stuck out a hand. "Edwin tells me you're looking for a place to settle down and open up a store." He raised a speculative eyebrow, "And that you just came across the desert on horseback—alone?"

Langely hadn't worked out all of the answers yet. As Lemont's eyes measured him, he sorted through what he had already said, careful to choose words that did not go crossways with what he had told the desk clerk, Edwin.

"I'm moving around," he admitted. "Maybe I'll settle down if I find what I'm looking for."

Lemont's gray head nodded. "Taking old Horace Greeley's advice, heh? What kind of business do you wish to open, Mr. Bracken?"

"Hardware." The lie was becoming easier. "In a growing land like this, people have a need for hardware. . . ."

Lemont had produced a pad and pencil from his pocket and was scribbling away. He looked up when Langely paused and begged forgiveness.

"Being owner, editor, distributor, and the *Gazette*'s only reporter, I find it necessary to glean news wherever I happen to stumble across it. Frankly, Mr. Bracken, news in Esteros Creek is often hard to stumble across—even in the dark!" He chuckled at his little joke. Edwin too. "If I don't jump on every turn of the screw, so to speak, I fear the *Esteros Creek Gazette* will become a thing of the past. You don't mind?"

"No," Langely said, but just the same he did mind.

"Now, you spell your name B-r-a-c-k-e-n?"

"Uh-huh."

"And you want to open up a hardware store?"

"If I find the right location. Folks working a new land like this are going to need tools."

"How true, how true," Lemont mumbled, touching the tip of his pencil to his tongue. "And you'll carry the usual line of goods?"

"Hammers, nails, saws, fencing, plows . . ."

Lemont looked up from his pad and cleared his

throat. "Ah, Mr. Bracken, I don't think I'll print what you just said about the plows and fences."

Langely's eyes hardened ever so slightly.

Lemont said, "You see, this is basically cattle country. Folks sort of have strong feelings on these things."

"They don't eat vegetables, Mr. Lemont?"

Lemont smiled thinly. "It is just that this is a bad time to be confronting certain people with this sort of thing. The local situation right at the moment. Precarious." Lemont fluttered his hand in the air and continued in a reassuring voice, "But it will blow over soon."

Langely changed the subject. "I was just on my way out to eat. Can a decent dinner be had in this town?"

Lemont's face brightened. "Might I recommend the La Casa Luna, down the street. If you like your food hot and spicy, you'll not find better."

Langely wasn't sure about hot and spicy, but he thanked Lemont. The editor thrust a folded newspaper at him. "A complimentary copy, Mr. Bracken. Read it at dinner."

He accepted the paper and Lemont's warm smile and left the two men chatting across the desk. Outside, the gray fingers of evening were stretching across the street. Shops were closing their doors for the day, legitimizing the hush that settled upon the town everywhere except the saloon. A dog barked someplace off in an alley. Up the street men hooted and howled, and the tinny sound of a piano drifted out from the swinging doors.

Langely stepped down to the street and angled across. As he climbed to the walk in front of the sheriff's office, he was keenly aware of the vacant spot on his hip and how his hand fell at his side when he walked—ready

—like a steel trap set to snap shut at the least provocation. That would have to change.

He moved the newspaper to the offending hand.

Passing the general store, he paused to look at the carriage still tied in front. Its polished wood and thick-pleated black-leather seats spoke of more money than he'd see in a lot of years tending a store—more than he could ever hope to come by through honest work. The horses were a matched pair. He looked them over and then eased nearer to the store windows and glanced inside.

Past a blackened potbelly stove, beyond the long wooden counter, he spied her. The girl from the carriage. A still life of simple beauty, he thought, framed in an open doorway and illuminated by the warm yellow glow of a kerosene lamp burning in the back room.

3

She carried herself with the proud, self-assured ease Langely had only rarely observed in an Indian among white men. And yet her penetrating obsidian eyes revealed more than just an Indian girl dressed in white man's clothing. She seemed a shining rose among cactus thorns. She didn't belong, and yet somehow she fitted in perfectly.

Standing in the doorway, gazing into the back room, she nodded her head and pointed now and then as if directing some activity. Then she touched her long black braid, pulled it over her shoulder, and absently wrapped it around her hand as she stepped away from the doorway to allow another woman to come through with a bolt of cloth clutched in her arms.

This second woman was young and blond. Her willowy figure made her appear almost too tall. She wore a simple white blouse with a high ruffled neck and three-quarter-length sleeves. Her brown skirt swept the floor as she walked, and when she set the bolt of material on the countertop, she said something witty that made her face burst apart in spontaneous laughter.

The darker girl fingered the texture of the cloth and made a comment that drew a nod of agreement. Then without warning, as if the Indian woman had sensed his presence out on the sidewalk, she glanced around and saw his face in the window. She looked quickly away and whispered to the other girl, who made a display of casualness as her carefully averted eyes glanced around the store to the front.

Langely realized that he was staring. He swung away from the window and continued up the street to the café.

The La Casa Luna was a long, narrow affair, dimly lit by rows of candle lamps flickering from wall niches carved into the adobe bricks above each of the tables. A few tables cluttered the center of the floor, and at the back a door separated the eating area from where the cooking was done. Out of long habit Langely chose a table against the wall. A bright-skirted woman in a dingy apron appeared promptly from the kitchen and spread a single page of wrinkled paper before him. The entrees all had a foreign sound to them, and Langely decided upon a dish that he hoped was chemically safe.

When she left, he unfolded the newspaper, but found that the Indian woman and her blond-haired friend crowded in on his thoughts. Lemont's paper forgotten, Langely pondered the finer qualities of Esteros Creek—other than the sparkling river and tall shade trees.

The Mexican woman broke his reverie with the steaming plate held between hot pads. He sectioned off a small portion of the doughy-cheesy concoction with the edge of his fork, blew on it, and tasted it. Somewhat spicy, but not bad. He cooled his mouth with a sip of water and tried it again.

After dinner Langely attempted the newspaper again, spreading it open on the table. The *Esteros Creek Gazette* was a four-page summary of social events, sprinkled liberally with gossip. Lemont had spoken truthfully when he said real news was rare! Plainly nothing of great significance happens in Esteros Creek, and that suited Thomas Langely just fine. The town was looking more and more inviting all the time.

Folding the final page and rolling it into a neat, thin tube, a word caught his eye.

Largo.

He opened the paper, pressing it flat on the table again, and read the short invitation welcoming the people of Esteros Creek to a coming-home party being thrown by the owner of the Largo Ranch, Martha Kincade, in honor of her daughter Valerie, recently returned home from an eastern college for women. Langely paused a moment to recall another name Edwin had mentioned. *The Double T.* Edwin had hinted at the trouble between them. Lemont made no mention of trouble in the article.

He tossed down the remainder of the coffee and paid for the meal. On the dark street outside he paused. Happy sounds drifted down from the Silver Lady Saloon. Someone was banging out a melody on an out-of-tune piano, and uninhibited voices wailed along. The saloon was alive—the only alive place in town—and it tugged his feet up the street toward the lights and friendly noises like a moth drawn to flame.

At the last moment he turned abruptly away from the swinging doors. He was a storekeeper—at least that's the story he was telling folks. His name was Thomas Bracken, he reminded himself. A respectable citizen in search of a respectable life. Rubbing elbows with drunk cowboys and ladies of dubious reputations was no way to start out in a new town. He stepped back out of the traffic of the busy sidewalk, poked a finger into a pocket on his vest for the plug of tobacco, and came up empty. Ruefully he started back toward the hotel.

The fancy carriage was no longer tied up in front of the general store when he strolled past. He thought of the two girls again and stopped, staring at the front door, which was still open. Hardly aware of the direction his feet were carrying him, he stepped through the dark entrance. A lamp in the back room pushed a rectangle of light out the doorway where earlier the Indian girl had stood, and a long shadow flickered across the far wall. Soft humming came to his ears; light, airy notes that reminded him of someone else—a long time ago. He put the memories back where they belonged and considered quietly retreating, when the girl suddenly appeared and stopped short seeing him standing there.

"Oh!" She backed up a step and composed herself. "You startled me," she said. "I didn't know anyone was here." Her eyes darted to the open door, then back. "I declare, if I don't remember to close that door, one of these days I'll leave the store open all night!"

"I didn't mean to startle you. I thought the store was still open."

"Well, I guess it is," she laughed, a little uncertainly, and looked back into his face. Her gaze narrowed. "Haven't I seen you somewhere?"

He grinned. "I don't know where you could have. I just rode into town a few hours ago. Never been in Esteros Creek before."

"But I'm sure I . . . yes, at the window, earlier—"

"Perhaps. I was window-shopping on my way to dinner." He had, in a certain respect, been window-shopping. Her scrutinizing stare made him wonder why he had stepped into the store anyway. Had he been so long under the desert sun that the sight of two pretty girls could draw him aimlessly into dark buildings?

She eased some then and smoothed the dark material of her long skirt nervously. "Then that explains it. Well, how can I help you?"

He thought quickly. "Tobacco. I seem to have run out."

"Chewing or smoking?"

"Chewing."

She reached in a hand to explore a dark bin. It came out empty. "I seem to be out too," she said. "But I have some in back." And she was gone.

He glanced around the store and found himself wondering what it would be like to really wait on customers and sell hardware. A low glass case along the wall drew his eye. Inside it a row of shiny revolvers decorated a carpet of green velvet. An 1851 Navy Colt there brought on a smile. His first gun had been a Navy. Beside it lay an 1873 Army Colt that could have been a twin to the one packed away in his saddlebags. A boyhood fascination with those nickel-plated and blue-steel weapons had first attracted him and beguiled him to follow the adventurous road, to visit the perilous grounds that he so desperately wanted to leave behind now. That he was good with a gun he couldn't help. He never tried to be. Some things just come naturally.

"Here you go. Mister . . . ?" Her voice drew the word into a question.

The darkness hid their color from him, but Langely was sure her eyes must be blue. Her golden hair glowed with a warm halo of lamplight from the back room.

"Bracken, ma'am. Thomas Bracken." The name stumbled from his mouth. He remembered his hat and snatched it off his head.

She glanced at the gun case, then back. "You aren't wearing a gun, Mr. Bracken. Are you interested in seeing one of those?" She reached for the display case.

He put out a hand. "No—no thanks. I wouldn't know what to do with a revolver if I had one. Probably end up shooting off my big toe or something."

She gave him a quick, shrewd glance. "A man who works cattle or travels much in the desert generally carries one. You look like you spend a lot of time on the back of a horse. Are you one of the Double T's new hands?"

Langely shook his head. "I just spent twenty days eating road dust, to be sure, ma'am, but I'm not a beef pusher. I'm a storekeeper." He felt wickedly deceptive, but he couldn't start a different yarn now. "I sold my hardware store back east and headed west. Other than my saddle carbine, which I haven't shot in the better part of a year and, I'm beginning to suspect, is an unnecessary encumbrance to my poor horse, I really have no use for a gun. Now, if you can show me a nice shotgun like a Purdy or a Greener and point me in the direction of a good bird dog, my bet is this valley with its tall grass is thick with quail."

She laughed, and a friendly smile warmed her face. "A storekeeper! Well, I'm very glad to meet you, Mr. Bracken. My name is Sarah Lawrence. I own this store." She offered her hand.

"Own?" Langely glanced at the naked fourth finger on her left hand. "The sign out front says, 'Joshua Lawrence.' You must be—"

"His daughter," she said quickly, averting her eyes. "Father died last winter. Now I run the store."

"I'm sorry." He looked around the building. "This is quite a large store, a lot for a young lady to run all by herself."

He felt the change come suddenly, the way one feels electricity in the air before a storm. "Not too big that I can't handle it," she said, her eyes instantly tempestuous. "Is there anything else you wanted, Mr. Bracken?"

He shook his head, dismayed. She marched to the cash drawer. "That will be ten cents for the tobacco."

The encounter ended as quickly as it had started, and once again Langely found himself standing on the dark sidewalk, listening to the tortured piano wailing away up the street, wondering what he had said to draw fire from Sarah Lawrence.

The sound of splintering wood and a rousing cheer brought his view up to the saloon as the batwing doors crashed apart and a man tumbled into the street. A stream of men flowed out behind him.

There was laughter and hooting and the waving of whiskey bottles as a tall, wide-built fellow with a belly beginning to crowd out his belt buckle pushed into the circle of men and hoisted a tottering old man by the shirtfront. "I'll learn you Largo people that you ain't welcome here," the big man said, and with a vicious suddenness drove a fist into the man's soft midsection.

Pushing the twist of tobacco into his vest pocket, Langely moved toward the circle of men. His hand brushed his side, and he remembered he was unarmed except for a short-blade knife tucked into the top of his boot, which didn't account for much in the way of weaponry. He reminded himself that he was here in Esteros Creek to stay out of trouble and that he was only now shouldering into this circle of men to satisfy his curiosity.

Unfortunately the old man groveling in the street had a face Langely recognized. So what if he had come within inches of running him over with that big fancy carriage? The old man had been quick with a friendly, apologetic smile, and there was his lovely companion too.

The chesty man standing over the old-timer was well oiled and filled with bottled courage. He was twenty years younger and fifty pounds heavier. He stood with legs spread and fist clenched, swaying a little from too much whiskey.

The old man spat blood and looked up from the dust.

The tall bully reached for him. "Get up, you son-of-a-sod-buster. I'll show you and that two-faced old woman you work for what people around here are really feeling."

The old man clutched his ribs. A trickle of blood creased his chin and dripped to his shirt collar. He tried to speak as the big man heaved him off the ground and the night air rang with a sharp crack of knuckles against bone.

Langely could detect no sympathy in the crowd, but

this wasn't his problem. When he left Montana, he left behind sticking his nose into other people's affairs, and he wasn't about to start all over again here.

With reluctance, he turned to leave. A bone crushing smack spun the old man around and dropped him back to the ground. Langely wheeled back, not liking what he knew he was about to do.

The big fellow lifted the old man off the ground and shoved him into the circle of onlookers. Someone caught him and tossed him across to another man. They laughed as the old man tumbled across again, then came whirling back and landed in Langely's arms.

He hung there, head lolled to one side, blood dripping from his nose and mouth onto Langely's sleeve.

"What are you waiting for?" someone yelled.

"We ain't done with the weasel yet. Toss him back," another voice sang out drunkenly.

He should have ignored the trouble right from the start. Should have returned to his hotel room, pulled down the window, and drew the curtains. He hadn't. His curiosity had dealt him a crooked hand, and now, with more than twenty pairs of eyes turned toward him, he was about to receive a fair share of whatever trouble was brewing. If only it wasn't that it was an old man . . . But the truth was, Langely could never abide surly bullies.

"He's all done in. Let him be," Langely said evenly, trying to sound reasonable about it, but knowing the challenging ring was there and knowing, too, that he could never hide it.

The chill night air grew silent. The bully adjusted his wide-leg stance and narrowed an eye at him. "You're a stranger in town, ain't you?"

Langely measured him in a glance. Although broader in the shoulders, he was no taller. Yet he cut a formidable figure in the light from the saloon door, his face shadowed by a broad, dark hat, a long-barreled six-gun on his side. Langely let the silence drag out.

"I guess you don't know which side o' the fence you're walking, mister," the man continued. "Just you drop that Largo skunk and I'll forget you ever got mixed up in this."

The offer was inviting. "Afraid I can't do that," Langely said, and his eyes hardened. He remembered other towns, and other men he had faced—and had left spilling their blood into the dust.

A stir rippled through the crowd. The man in the center of the ring released the hammer thong on his pistol.

"He ain't wearing a gun, Hank," someone said.

"Give him yours," the bully barked.

A cowboy unbuckled his gun belt and shoved it at him. Langely ignored it. "He's an old man. You'll end up killing him."

"The only thing more deserving of a beating than a Largo skunk is a nose-butting stranger." Hank raised a finger and pointed at the gun. "You can either take that gun and die with it, or die without it!"

Someone jerked the old man from his arms, and the circle fanned out. Hank waited, fingers tense above the pistol on his hip.

Liquor makes men brave. It puts bold words in their mouths and ties an anchor to their reflexes. Langely knew that, just as certainly as he knew what would follow next if he took that gun. This Hank fellow was a dead man already. But then it would start all over again

—the back watching, the steady parade of fast-hand kids itching to make a name for themselves. He didn't need that. He'd had his fill of it up north, but to die on a strange street in a strange town was no way to handle the problem. Alive, he could ride out; other towns waited. He could try again somewhere else.

Reluctantly Thomas Langely reached for the holster.

4

The sharp crack of a rifle shot shattered the tight-breath silence. She levered a fresh shell into the Winchester with the same smoothness that another woman might pull a comb through her hair, and narrowed an eye over the sights.

Her words rang sharp and clear, with no hint of the accent that Thomas Langely somehow thought would be there. "Drop that gun belt, Hank Acker, or so help me, the next bullet will go through your rotten heart!"

Acker's eyes changed. Langely saw it, and his fingers itched for that gun now. She had picked the wrong man and the wrong time—too many people were enjoying Acker's dilemma. It twisted like a knife in his pride.

Acker spread his hands. "Take it easy with that rifle, little lady." A mixture of curiosity and amusement played on the faces of the men standing about. He grinned to hide his own embarrassment. "It might accidentally go off."

"If it goes off, it won't be by accident. Now, drop your gun!"

"Okay, lady, we all know you can shoot, but I ain't dropping my gun for no squaw!"

She tightened the rifle to her shoulder. "You have no choice."

Langely winced. Her words sounded vaguely like the ultimatum Acker had given him a few minutes earlier.

More townspeople gathered along the sidewalk. Hank Acker wiped away a trickle of perspiration from the corner of his eye, and his hand lowered toward the revolver at his side.

"Break it up, break it up!" a voice ordered, and the man behind it pushed into the crowd. As he moved, the thin light from the saloon glinted off the star on his vest. He was well on in years and a good half head shorter than Acker, but he faced the bully unflinchingly and said, "Give me that revolver."

Acker shoved the gun into his hand as if it had just come off a smithy's forge, anxious to be rid of it to a man instead of surrendering to the woman. The sheriff turned to the woman then. "Put up the rifle, Valerie."

When she didn't move at once, he said, "Well, what are you waiting for, put it up before you hurt someone."

"He beat Joe to an inch of his life, Burt, and he was about to gun down an unarmed man!" The rifle remained pointed at Acker.

"It's all over, Val," the sheriff said patiently. "Put up the rifle."

She hesitated a moment longer, then snapped the gun off her shoulder and knelt beside the old man. She said to Langely, "Will you please help me get Joe off the street?"

The sheriff wheeled back to Acker. "The next time you feel like bullying somebody, leave the old men and women out of it, hear? You'll find plenty of young bucks happy to go a few rounds with you."

"I hear you, Jenney. Next time no old men or squaws," he said glancing at Langely. "How about my gun?"

"It will be waiting for you in my office when you're ready to leave town. Now, get out of here before I change my mind and throw you in jail for the night."

Acker marched back into the saloon, and a stream of cowboys broke away from the crowd and trickled after him. Jenney said to the crowd, "The excitement's over, folks, go on home." Then he looked at the old man on the ground and grinned. "You're a might old for barroom brawling, ain't you, Joe? Don't you know that's for younger men?" He laughed and hunkered down beside him, but Langely saw the look of concern on his face and heard it in his voice. "How are you feeling?"

Joe shook his head. "I hurt real bad, Burt. The boy busted a couple ribs." He gave a faint smile then. "But I'll be okay. Been through a lot worse in the old days, eh."

"You sure have, Joe. Like the time I carried you out of the Silver Lady so as Doc could cut two slugs out of your hide. Come to think of it, you always did come out on the short side of a fight."

Joe laughed and gripped his side. "Sometimes wonder how I made it this far. Suppose the good Lord is keeping me around for a reason?"

"You're just too ornery to die." Jenney looked at Langely. "I don't know you."

"He tried to help Joe," Valerie said.

"Is that right?"

"I happened to be in the right place at the wrong time," Langely said.

Burt studied him in the meager light from the Silver Lady Saloon. "It's fortunate you're not packing iron. Hank Acker's mighty handy with a six-shooter when he's in one of his rollicking moods." The sheriff extended his hand. "Burt Jenney."

Langely took it and gave him his new name. Out the corner of his eye he saw Sarah Lawrence coming up the street. He said, "We best get him to a doctor."

"Doc Lester is out to the Callahans' place tonight, Lilly's expecting . . . again," Jenney said.

"We need to get him off the street," Valerie said.

Sarah stopped at Valerie's side and looked down at Joe. Lines of concern deepened in her forehead. "I've got a cot in my back room."

Langely and Jenney carried Joe into the general store and lowered him onto the cot. Burt said, "Since Joe's in good hands now, I'll be leaving. Need to get back out in the street."

"Aren't you going to do anything about Hank Acker?"

Jenney frowned. "I'll go have a talk with him, Val, but some men . . ." He shook his head to indicate the futility of it all.

Sarah filled a pot of water and carried it to the stove. "For a man fresh into town, Mr. Bracken, you sure make yourself known right away," she said coolly.

"That seems to be my fate."

Her eyes narrowed, searching for meaning in that. She nodded at the stove. "There's a stack of wood out back, do you mind . . . ?"

He wondered what it was he had said earlier to draw out her wrath. His words at the time had seemed innocent enough. In the lamplight he saw that her eyes were indeed blue, very blue—pretty eyes—how incongruous for a woman with so fiery a temper.

Out behind the store the night air was turning cool, and he inhaled deeply, as if that would clear the dust of the street from his nostrils. Through the dark trees he heard the river flowing nearby. It was a pleasant sound, and for a moment his thoughts strayed back to Montana and the trees and water he had left behind. But that was old ground. He found the woodpile and stacked quarters in the crook of his arm as his mind turned to the other towns he had known. Trouble seemed to follow him like wolves after a wounded animal. Up north he expected it, he watched for it. His reputation had been plastered across the front pages of newspapers from Kalispell to Sheridan, and he could count on some fast-hand, wet-behind-the-ear kid to try and take it from him.

That was a thousand miles away. People didn't know him here in Esteros Creek, and still they were bent on sticking a gun in his fist. First Sarah Lawrence, then Hank Acker . . . and he'd only been in town three hours.

He loaded his arms with wood and carried it inside. Marcus Lemont was there. The newspaperman glanced up from the pad where he was scribbling—the next edition of the *Esteros Creek Gazette* would have a real headline, Langely mused.

"Well, well, Mr. Bracken, what a surprise." Lemont glanced at Valerie. "My dear, is this the Good Samaritan that came to Joe in his hour of need?"

She nodded.

"A mighty act of bravery," he pronounced, filling the room with a slight odor of whiskey. "Yes, brave indeed, facing a dangerous man like Hank Acker . . ."

"Dangerous to old men and young ladies," Langely said. He looked at Valerie. "And from what I saw tonight, he'd better stick with the old men."

"Well said, well said, my boy, may I quote you?" Lemont had his pencil going again.

Langely made a wry smile. "I'd rather you didn't."

Valerie glanced from Langely to Lemont. "You know this man?"

Lemont flicked his hand at the insignificance of the matter. "We met briefly in the foyer"—he used the French pronunciation—"of the Montgomery earlier this evening. Mr. Bracken is quite an extraordinary store-keeper. He rides clear across the desert—alone—to our splendid little valley, then takes an evening stroll and ends up facing one of the territory's top guns—unarmed! Eastern storekeepers must be a brave breed of men!"

Sarah gave a short laugh and said, "It sounds more like foolhardy."

Lemont chuckled. "And then we have the hot-tempered one—a purveyor of merchandise also." He grinned and bowed, flourishing a hand in her direction. "The little lady with the big store—"

"Lemont," Sarah warned, hefting a length of cord wood. "You keep a civil tongue in that head of yours, or what happened to Joe tonight will be nothing compared with what I'll do to you."

"Good Lord, give the dying some peace and quiet," Joe croaked from the cot.

Sarah wheeled on him. "You ain't about to die, Joe Lascoe, so don't look for more sympathy than you deserve!" She spun away, glared at Lemont, and went back to the stove and flung kindling into the firebox.

Lemont chuckled and winked at Langely. "A hot-blooded filly, that one is," he whispered. "Just waiting for the right man to come along and break her."

Langely wanted no part of that job.

Valerie sat by Joe and patted his forehead with a damp cloth. Langely remembered the newspaper article and was mildly surprised at discovering that the daughter of Martha Kincade—a name as American as apple pie—had a face as Indian as that Chiricahua Apache down south who was causing such a fuss down along the border.

"Where do you keep the bandages?" Langely asked, deciding to make himself useful.

Sarah nodded to the cupboard without looking at him. "You'll find some in there. If you need more, I have them out front."

He located them and, with Valerie's help, wrapped Joe's bruised chest. Joe endured the pain without fuss. When they finished, Sarah said, "Water's boiling, Joe. Can I fix you some tea?"

"Tea?" Joe roared with displeasure. His face screwed up into a knot of anguish. "What I need is something to kill the pain!"

"Ah . . . !" Lemont leaped from the chair he had retreated to after Sarah's cord-wood advance and sat on the corner of the cot. He peeled back his top coat and removed a shiny silver flask. "I have just the elixir to rejuvenate a weary soul," he said, unscrewing the silver cap.

Joe Lascoe's eyes brightened. He hitched himself up on his elbow despite a stabbing pain that made him wince and said, "Lemont, you sure have a hell of a way of saying what's on your mind, but I do admire your deep understanding of a fellow's needs."

Joe took a sip, smacked his lips, and passed it back to Lemont. Langely caught Valerie's eyes watching him. She blinked and looked away.

"Can I get you some tea, Miss Kincade?" he asked.

Behind him Sarah exclaimed, "Oh, I'm so thoughtless, you must be exhausted. I swear, I don't know why Burt lets such a man walk the streets." She filled a teacup and handed it to Valerie. "Hank Acker would have thought nothing of shooting you down, just as he was about to do to Mr. Bracken before you came to his aid."

Langely winced at the remark.

Valerie wrapped her fingers around the warm cup and allowed him to help her into the chair Lemont had abandoned.

"All of a sudden I feel so tired," she said, putting the back of her hand to her forehead. "I've never pointed a gun at a man before. I used to hunt with my father, but it's not at all the same. I mean, pointing a gun at an animal is one thing, but a man, that's something else again. And you know what really scares me?" She looked deeply into his gray eyes as if trying to search out his soul. "What really frightens me is that if Burt had not come when he did, I know I would have killed that man." She turned away, her face hardening. "I didn't know I had it in me. God, I hate this land! You live and act like animals to survive, and become no better than the people who torment you."

She looked at Langely. "Do you know what it's like to almost kill a man, Mr. Bracken?"

Sarah laughed. "That's certainly not the kind of question to ask Mr. Bracken. Handguns scare him, you see; he's afraid he might shoot off a big toe . . . or something."

Langely wanted to tell Sarah what killing really felt like, but he held his tongue. Storekeepers generally didn't know much about such things. He snatched his hat off the table and said to Valerie, "You'll be wanting to get back to your home soon, I should think. Considering the circumstances, that will be the best place for you. Joe won't be much good for a couple of days, so if you'd like, I'll drive you out in the morning."

"That's very kind of you, Mr. Bracken, but I wouldn't want to put you to any more trouble on our account. If people start associating you with the Largo, it can make life hard here in Esteros Creek."

"My guess is that I'm already associated," he said. "Double-T wranglers are probably drawing lots for my hide right now. Most of the town turned out to watch, so I wouldn't worry too much about ruining my reputation. Besides, I'd feel better knowing you got back home safely."

She glanced down at her dress and smoothed an imagined wrinkle. "All right, Mr. Bracken, you may drive Joe and me back to the ranch. We can take a hotel room for tonight?"

Sarah said, "You'll do nothing of the kind. You and Joe will stay here with me tonight."

"In the morning, then." Langely took his eyes from Valerie and glanced at Joe and Lemont—both men intent on emptying the silver flask. He felt Sarah Lawrence's singeing glare upon his back as he turned and ducked out the door.

"Mr. Bracken, Mr. Bracken—just a moment."

He drew up as the newspaper editor came out into the street. "Is something the matter?"

"Matter? Matter? Why nothing's the matter, my boy. A favor—when you return from the Largo, I'd appreciate it if you'd stop by and see me in my office—ah, a personal thing." He grinned.

The friendly face offered no clue. Lemont was probably a hell of a poker player, Langely decided. "Sure, when I return."

"Good . . . good, I'll see you then." Lemont turned away and hurried back into the store.

Langely paused in the shadow of the Montgomery Hotel to listen to the piano music drifting up the street. Valerie Kincade was a mystery, Lemont a sly old buzzard that deserved watching, and Sarah Lawrence . . . ? The thought of her both intrigued and nettled him. She worked so hard at being hostile, and yet, he knew, something quite different churned just beneath the surface, something he couldn't quite put a finger on. Oddly, thinking of her brought a smile to his lips.

The piano stopped playing, a roar of laughter erupted, and it started up again on a different tune. The dark street was empty and quiet but for whatever noise came from the saloon, and that would probably go on all night.

5

"Damn Indian squaw!" Acker threw the whiskey down his throat and banged the empty glass on the table.

Brad Manning glanced up from the deck he was shuffling and said, "Forget it, Hank. There was no way you could have known she was there with a rifle."

Acker's fist whitened around the glass. "That squaw made a fool of me in front of the whole town. I can't easily forget that!" He swung toward the bar and called for another drink. "I'll tell you what, it's a sorry day when a white man's got to take that from an Indian, 'specially a squaw Indian!"

The men around the table murmured their agreement as Brad Manning tossed the cards into five piles. Acker gathered in his hand and studied the marks, but his thoughts were elsewhere.

Harve Winter called for three cards and said, "I sure didn't see her come up from behind like she done."

"Injuns are like that," Sam Levi said around the pipe clenched in his teeth. "I'll take two." He discarded a pair onto the table. "I remember back in 'sixty-two," he went on, sliding the new cards among those in his fingers, "while most folks back east were fighting each other, we was fighting the Kiowa. That was back when Big Jim Kincade was still alive, before the Double T and the Largo had their disagreement. We cleaned them red hides out of this country real good, made it safe for cattle and white folks—but I'll tell you what, when you're up in them hills and a heap of them red bucks are out to take your scalp, you don't never hear 'em! Makes my fur ruffle to think of it even now!"

"Things would be different today if Jim Kincade was still alive," Harve said sullenly.

Calvin Dexter looked up. Calvin's roots went way back, back before Big Jim Kincade and Thaddeus Tyrell came to the valley and staked claim to two of the biggest cow camps in the territory—back before the dusty Spanish settlement of Esteros Creek even had a name. "I don't know that that's true," he said thoughtfully. "Jim and Martha usually saw eye to eye on most things, if I remember 'em right." He laughed. "Quite a pair they made. Stubborn as a bear in a beehive, both of 'em. No, I kinda think if Jim Kincade was alive today, things would still be pretty much as they are, 'cept that Mr. Tyrell would have a lot more to contend with than a tired old lady."

"What ever did start that trouble between Kincade and Tyrell?" Harve asked.

Calvin shrugged. "Lots o' things, boy. It was a tension that took years to develop, but the straw that broke

T. Tyrell's back was when Big Jim decided to dam up the Porter. The Porter had been good water for Tyrell's northern range, and it rankled the old man when Kincade cut it off."

"You want cards, Calvin?" Brad asked.

"Naw, I'll stick with these," the old-timer said.

"How about you, Hank?"

Lisa Wingate drifted over to the table and set the glass of rye whiskey by Acker's elbow. She slid a hand over his shoulder. "Which one of you boys is winning?" she asked, softly stroking their faces with large, playful brown eyes.

Brad grinned at Lisa. "Just started, honey, but stick around."

Calvin chuckled and winked at Lisa. "You wait till I play out this hand, darlin', and I'll buy the whole house a drink."

Lisa left Acker's side, waltzed behind Calvin, and combed her fingers through his wispy gray hair. "That good?" she asked, leaning over his shoulder for a look.

Brad glanced over at Acker. "Well, do you want cards?"

Acker rocked back in his chair, looking but not seeing the black-and-red marks in his hand. He threw them on the table and kicked back his chair. "I can't get my mind on the game. You boys play without me," he said, and snatched up his drink.

Brad threw in his hand and proclaimed a misdeal.

"Damn!" Calvin shook his head and spread out an ace-high full house. "Wouldn't you know it," he said.

Lisa ruffled his hair. "Sorry old-timer, better luck next time." And she moved off to another table.

* * *

Acker made his way through the tables scattered about the smoke-filled saloon to the bar and shouldered himself between two men who were standing there.

"Whiskey, and leave the bottle," he said when the bartender came by. He looked sideways at one of the men. "Well, what are you two staring at, Canon?"

Albert Canon grinned. "If I was you, Hank, I'd get rid of that holster. It looks kind of funny hanging there all empty like it is."

"If I was you, Canon, I'd keep my mouth shut. It'd look kind of funny all full of broken glass and missing teeth after I shove this bottle down it."

"Calm down Hank," Sidney Lowe said at his left. A thin smile widened across his face, and his pale eyes glistened with the warmth of a December blizzard. "Al didn't mean nothing. You couldn't help what happened tonight. That Injun got the drop on you when your back was turned. It wasn't a fair fight."

"Yeah, that's the way them Injuns are—sneaky." Canon said.

"We was just talking 'bout it," Lowe went on. "You can't let what happened tonight go by. I mean, we need to show folks that if they push around Double T hands, somebody will push back."

Canon toyed with his glass. "What do you plan to do about it, Hank?"

"I don't know. Haven't given it much thought." Acker contemplated his reflection in the long mirror behind the neatly tiered triangles of glasses. After a moment of speculation he grinned. "That squaw ain't so wild as I can't tame her down a mite. I got a notion what I'd like to do to that little blanket warmer." He gulped down the rest of his drink, and Lowe promptly refilled the glass.

"Now you're talking sense. Canon and me, we figured you'd have something like that in mind, so we've been making plans."

Acker glanced at the shorter man. "What kind of plans?"

Lowe said, "That girl and the old man will be driving back to the Largo in the morning. The way you worked the old buzzard over, he's in no condition to cause us any trouble. The Injun will be easy pickin's." Lowe grinned. "It's a long road between town and that ranch."

Canon added, "We can get a half-dozen men and wait for them in the cottonwoods down where the road crosses the Old River."

Acker thought this over and drained the glass in a single swallow. "Yeah, we could do that." He rubbed a hand under his bristled chin and stared bleary-eyed at the legion of bottles that marched along a ledge in front of the mirror. His eyes brightened then. "Sounds kinda good to me."

Acker grabbed up the bottle, filled their glasses, and sent more rye whiskey surging down his throat. "Let's do it!"

Lowe glanced over at Canon, grinned, and said to Acker, "Now that that's settled, what are we going to do about the stranger?"

"Stranger?" Acker frowned. "He ain't important. Some no-account drifter that got mixed up in something he should have left alone. Forget him."

"We got to think about the reputation of the Double T. Can't let strangers step on our toes and get away with it like he done."

Acker considered this, staring at the amber flash in his fingers where the whiskey glass caught the lamplight. "Yeah, reputation," he mumbled, but his brain, already knee-deep in eighty-proof brew, was occupied with thoughts of a more tantalizing nature than a mere foot-loose drifter. Valerie Kincade, the high and mighty Indian girl, raised in a big house on a big ranch, educated in fancy schools back east. Too good for just any white man. *Well, little miss high and mighty, if I can't come up to your level, I can damn well drag you down to mine!*

Acker drained his glass. "I don't care about the stranger. Do whatever you think best."

Lowe said, "We was figuring that Canon and a couple boys will work him over in the morning—just to teach him a lesson about minding his own business. And I'll round up six or seven riders. We can leave at daybreak so we don't miss them. . . ."

Lowe glanced up at the mirror, and his words trailed off. Acker became aware of the man standing behind them too. Burt Jenney pushed between them and ordered a beer.

The sheriff tasted the foamy head, licked his lips, and turned to look out over the crowded saloon. "You boys ought to be more careful who you let overhear your private conversations," he said.

Acker turned back to the bar and gazed at the rows of evenly stacked glasses. "I didn't much care for you taking my gun like you did, Burt."

Jenney laughed. "Don't be a fool, Acker. What did

you expect me to do in front of all those people? Come on, let's find someplace where we can talk."

The four men moved from the bar to a table in the corner.

6

The coming dawn was smudged pink against the black horizon as Dave Thompson rode into the courtyard on a fast horse and reined to a sliding halt. In the early-morning mist that settled like a shroud about the rambling house, he swung down and in a quick motion turned the reins around the worn hitching rail. He took the steps two at a time, uneasy at the urgency that would make Martha Kincade send the boy, Manuel, out to the line shack in the middle of the night to fetch him. Within the big house, lamps burned. Their yellow light fell from the windows across the dark porch outside, and Dave had a feeling they had been lit all night. As he mounted the porch, the door opened, and Martha Kincade appeared in a slanting oblong of light.

"Mrs. Kincade," he said, removing his hat as he entered the house. Martha Kincade was fully dressed, and Dave frowned. They were the same clothes she had had on the day before. He stepped past her into the large, brick-floor living room, expecting to find Valerie there. She wasn't. "Manuel said it was urgent," he said, turning back.

Martha Kincade's white blouse was buttoned tightly around her neck, her long sleeves fastened at the wrist. She was wearing a riding skirt. She always wore riding skirts, although Dave could not remember the last time he had seen Martha upon a horse. He noted a dark coffee stain on the front of her blouse—strikingly out of place with the woman's usual crisp appearance.

For all her sixty-two years Martha Kincade maintained a slim, sturdy figure. She wore her white hair wrapped up in a bun at the back of her head, but her appearance was that of a woman twenty years younger. Her skin, steadfastly protected from the fierce New Mexico sun by wide-brimmed hats whenever she ventured out of doors, was still tight and youthful—except around her blue eyes and at the corners of her mouth, where crow's feet etched deep furrows. Martha Kincade was no stranger to hardship, a woman forged of steel when need be. Despite a medical condition of late that had kept her bedridden for long periods at a stretch, she remained a woman to be reckoned with.

She closed the heavy door and stopped two feet from her foreman to face him as a man might. It was not in Martha's nature to beat around the bush. "Yesterday morning Valerie and Joe Lascoe went into town for supplies. They were supposed to be back last night." She turned away and gazed across the wide room toward the bay windows. "Dave, I've been worried sick all night."

"They're probably just delayed, Mrs. Kincade, and decided to wait till the morning."

Martha nodded her head. "I suspect you're right, Dave. I've been telling myself not to worry, but we've had so much trouble with the Double T as of late that, well, I just let my imagination get the best of me." Martha turned back. "You know how dependable Joe is. If he said he'd be back last night, come hell or high water, he'd be here!"

Dave Thompson had never known Martha Kincade to have misgivings about using profane language in the company of her men. It was a way of life when dealing with ranch business. When Valerie was present, however, such language was never tolerated. Martha had strict notions about what a *lady* was supposed to be— the *lady* Valerie Kincade had become.

Dave knew that when Jim had been alive, Martha secretly feared Valerie might revert back to the wild young thing that she knew was hiding within the girl's Indian blood. Jim had been a man's man. A man without a son to bestow his attentions on. He'd often forget, or just plain ignore, that Valerie was a girl and would treat her like a son. But after Jim's death Martha Kincade regained full control of the rearing and reshaping of her daughter.

Martha crossed the room to the large bay windows that faced the courtyard, which were graying with the advent of dawn.

Dave watched the old lady's back in the smoky light of the overhead lamps. He had known this woman almost twenty-five years. After Big Jim's death Martha took hold of the reins of the Largo and directed the affairs of the sprawling ranch as best she could. Though some men resented working for a woman, Dave had not. He stuck by her when other men started to look for jobs where men did the hiring and firing.

Then money got tight. Dave had had to let most of the remaining help go. It hurt him to do so, and it hurt the ranch. What men he could keep on had their hands full just preventing the dwindling herd from wandering onto Double T land or being run off by those that saw easy pickings. Dave regretted seeing the ranch falter. With the herds growing smaller and bills mounting, loans were drawn from the bank and papers signed. But when the loans came due, Martha had no money. She was forced down the only road open to her—selling off valuable bottom land to the hordes of farmers moving into the territory. She didn't like it any more than anyone else, but what choice did she have? Valerie was attending an expensive school back east, and Martha would sooner starve than deprive her daughter of that education.

"You want me to get some boys together and ride into town after them?" Dave asked.

"I'm probably being a foolish old woman, but I'd feel so much better knowing some Largo hands were near to help if they needed it."

"I'll leave right away," Dave said. He strode to the door to let himself out, stopped, and looked back at Martha Kincade, small and alone in the big house. The washed-out light of dawn through the bay windows turned her drawn face a chalky gray. Dave knew a pang of apprehension over the old woman's health. Martha tried too hard to be the same person she had been twenty years ago. Outside she might pass for a woman in her forties, but inside she was old. In the last six months her energies had seemed diminished, and now she stayed close to the house, sometimes spending days on end in bed. The doctor said it was exhaustion, but Dave knew it went far deeper than that. He glanced outside as the sun broke over the tops of the hills and he had a peculiar feeling about the day that was coming.

"Ma'am," he said, "why don't you try to get some rest. I'll see that everything is taken care of."

"I can't sleep, Dave, not now . . . maybe later."

Dave understood. He closed the door behind him and led his horse across the yard to the bunkhouse. Only twelve men slept within its walls now, but when Big Jim Kincade had built it, more than thirty bunks held as many wranglers. Those had been pleasant days.

The men were already rolling out of their beds, stirring about stocking-footed, getting the cook stove lighted, when Dave came through the door. "Get your pants on, boys," he said. "I need five riders. John, Larry, Edgar, Billy, and your brother, Ted. Get dressed and saddled up, you can eat when we get to Esteros Creek."

"What's up, Dave?" Bill Tremely asked, hobbling one-legged while poking the other into his pants.

"It's Valerie and Joe. They went into town yesterday and haven't come back. Mrs. Kincade wants us to find out why."

"Think they ran into trouble?"

Dave rubbed the worn walnut grip of the revolver on his side. "I hope not, but just the same, you better bring your guns." He drew his revolver and replaced three spent shells left unattended since the day before when he happened upon a prairie rattler curled in the sun alongside the line shack.

The sun was but a few degrees off the horizon when

they rode away from the big house. Dave saw the old woman watching from the window as they galloped under the adobe portals and out onto the road that led to town.

7

Langely slept more lightly than usual, coming awake throughout the night at the unfamiliar creaks and groans of new surroundings, and the sun was but a stain of rose-colored light spreading above a gray horizon when a sound brought him fully awake.

He lay for a moment beneath the sheets, not moving, not yet sure what had pulled him from his sleep. Then he heard the voices on the street below, and the knocking of a fist against a door. His eyes opened. He threw off the sheets and moved aside a corner the thin curtains across the open window.

Down on the street four riders waited in front of Burt Jenney's office. Hank Acker was standing by the closed jailhouse door. He knocked again, and a moment later the door opened. Acker stepped inside and reappeared on the sidewalk in another minute, shoving his pistol into his holster. He swung into the saddle, and the five men rode up the quiet street, crossed the wooden bridge at the end of town, and struck out on the north road.

Langely let the curtain fall back in place, recalling last night's trouble. A frown confronted him in the mirror as he dressed and combed the knots from his hair.

Edwin was whistling happily, polishing the oak counter top when Thomas Langely came down the stairs. "Morning, Mr. Bracken. Sleep well?"

"Like a log, Edwin," he said, stretching the truth some for the desk clerk's sake. "This western air is good for a man."

"It's the dryness. It keeps the lungs from filling up with . . . with what Doc Lester calls bad humors"— Edwin made a face—"or something like that." He shrugged his round shoulders. "Don't ask me what that means. I understand you had yourself a busy night, Mr. Bracken."

"Some fellows had too much to drink, that's all."

"It's a shame when a gentleman like yourself gets himself badgered by drunk and unruly troublemakers. I hope this won't change your mind about our town. Except for every now and then when someone needs to blow off a little steam, Esteros Creek is really a nice, quiet place."

Langely thought of the meager newspaper he had read the day before in the café after dinner, and then, quite unexpectedly, he was thinking of Sarah Lawrence. He gave Edwin a wry smile. "Perhaps last night was one of those rare occasions. From the little I've seen of Esteros Creek, I do believe it might be just what I'm looking for," he said cryptically.

A heavy burden seemed to rise from Edwin's sagging

shoulders. "I'm certainly glad to hear that, Mr. Bracken."

Langely nodded out the door at the street. "Which direction from town is the Double T Ranch?"

"That spread is down south, about ten miles or so. If you're planning to visit, I would not recommend it."

"Why's that?"

"Those men last night, they were from the Double T."

"What's up north?"

"Nothing but a lot of grass and a few trees—and of course the Largo. But that place is about fifteen miles out. Why do you ask?"

"If I'm going to make your little town my little town, I'd better get a feel for the lay of things. Maybe I'll ride out and look the countryside over."

"Better buy yourself a gun, then," Edwin said dolefully. "The land is full of snakes, the kind that crawl and the kind that walk on two legs."

Langely grinned to himself as he left. Five of those two-legged variety were probably curling up along the road somewhere between Esteros Creek and the Largo Ranch right now.

The morning was not yet hot enough to be uncomfortable as he stepped down to the powder-fine dust and climbed to the sidewalk across the street. Sarah's store was still locked up tight, as were most all the businesses at this early hour. At the La Casa Luna the aroma of frying eggs and bacon made his stomach protest. Nevertheless Langely postponed the urge to turn in and continued on to the livery.

The wide doors of the saloon were flung open to the

morning air as he strolled past. Inside, the diehards of last night's revelry lay sleeping across tables. A drowsy old man in a long white apron swept the floors around their feet while two young boys gathered up, emptied, and polished the brass spittoons.

Langely was keenly aware of the absence of the gun on his hip and found his hand lingering from habit by his side as he walked. He wondered if trying to change his life was worth the effort. Had he worn a gun last night, Hank Acker would be dead, and most likely he'd be waking up behind bars this morning. Instead he was free. Free to walk the streets of Esteros Creek under a clear morning sky. Free to get on his horse and ride wherever the spirit moved him, or free not to—

Considering all this as he strolled along the quiet street, listening to the morning birds and an occasional clip-clop of a passing horse, he decided the price wasn't too high to pay. He redoubled his determination to see this thing through no matter how hard folks tried to force a gun into his fist.

The shadow of the tall livery stable slashed across the street. Inside, he saddled his horse and was leading the animal out the big double doors when he spied the shiny carriage with its polished yellow-spoked wheels.

"That buggy over there belongs to the Kincades," he said to a boy raking out a stall. "There is two bits in it for you if you hitch up the team and drive it over to the general store."

"Sure thing, mister."

Langely flipped the boy a coin and rode back down the bright street.

In front of the barbershop he reined in. An OPEN sign hung in the window, and a man in a striped apron was sweeping a cloud of dust out the door. Langely rubbed his chin and nudged his horse to the hitching rail.

The man looked up from his sweeping. "Morning, mister."

"I need a shave, and a bath—if the water is hot."

"The missus starts stoking the boiler five o'clock every morning," the man said amiably. "Got more hot water than a fellow could use in a month of baths."

Considering how badly he smelled, Thomas Langely figured that to be just about enough.

8

Langely scrubbed a week's worth of trail dust from his body. The porcelain tub was a far cry from the dirt tank he'd last bathed in along the trail, but from the color the water had turned, it was hard to tell the difference. He soaked luxuriously in the warm water, and disdained the thought of crawling back into his filthy clothes. His next stop, when he had more time, would be a laundry. When he emerged from the back room, the barber was stropping a razor. The barber motioned to a chair and started brushing lather on his chin.

"Just get into town, mister?"

"Yesterday afternoon."

"I guess you was on hand for that fight we had last night."

"I did happen to see that."

"It's getting so a decent man or woman ain't safe on the street after dark."

The razor skimmed lightly over his cheek. "The desk clerk at the Montgomery Hotel says it was just some fellows blowing off a little steam."

"Edwin?" The barber snorted. "He don't see the world as most folks see it. To Edwin everyone is good. Even the bad have good in 'em."

"Most folks do."

"Not like Edwin sees it," the barber went on. "To Edwin bad people are really good people making a mistake."

"Wasn't it some sort of problem between two ranches?"

"Sure was. The Double T and the Largo. Been trouble between those two cow camps for a lot of years," he said. "I'll tell you what, mister. If it was up to me, I'd get them two outfits together, fill their hands with guns, and let 'em have at it. When the smoke cleared away, I'd just let the buzzards come and have themselves a feast on the bodies. I ain't got no love for the Double T with its wild, gun-happy firebrands shooting up the town. Or that Largo, and Old Lady Kincade parceling out bits and pieces of it to the farmers. That's what started the whole beehive a-buzzing again, you know.

"That woman is too old to run a cow camp nearly as big as some states back east, and she's too mule-brained to let someone younger than herself take it over. She's trying to hold on to more than half a million acres of land with no more than a bare-bone skeleton of a crew. The place ain't making no money. Martha Kincade's been borrowing from the bank to keep it going for years. Everyone knows that. And when the loans come due, she sells off the unmortgaged parcels to the sod busters. . . . You ain't a farmer, are you mister?"

"Wouldn't know which end of a plow to stick in the ground. Why don't the other ranches just buy her out?"

"Well," the barber went on, working the razor over Langely's face. "I reckon the only one wealthy enough to do that is Thaddeus Tyrell, and Old Lady Kincade would sooner give it to the devil than sell out to him!"

"Why's that?"

"The trouble between those two ranches goes deeper than just the trickle of land filling the farmer's pot," the barber said. "It goes way back—I reckon no one will ever know for sure what started it, since Jim Kincade is dead and Tyrell ain't talking about it. Folks say it began sometime after the war.

"It festered and brewed into a range war—not a big war, but bloody as hell. Shortly after the fighting stopped, Big Jim Kincade and a bunch of his hands—that old man got beat up last night, Joe Lascoe?—he was one of 'em—came riding into town. Tyrell was drinking in the old Silver Lady . . . it burned down in 'eighty-one, you know, that's when they built the new saloon. Well, Tyrell had a handful of his boys with him, and I guess words were spoke, 'cause the next thing you know, they went to shooting at each other. Jim was killed, and Martha holds Tyrell responsible. No one knows what started it, not even old Joe. When the gunsmoke cleared, the doctor managed to save two of 'em, Joe Lascoe and Thaddeus Tyrell. The rest he sent packing off to Strathmore's.

"Tyrell got shot up real bad. The doc said he'd never walk again, and that was the gospel truth. Mr. Tyrell rides in a buggy these days, with a pair of them walking sticks by his side. For the most part he just stays in that big stone house of his on the Double T.

"In a way it's a shame what happened between those two men. They came out west together, built up their places together, fought off the Kiowas together, and in the end fought each other."

"Why does Martha Kincade blame Tyrell for her husband's death?"

"It's sort of peculiar," the barber went on thoughtfully. "When they hauled Kincade out of the saloon that night, the only bullet hole in him was one in Big Jim's back, and it weren't no common bullet that made it, neither. It was one of them new factory-made cartridge bullets. Nowadays that's all you see, but right after the war they were mighty rare. Men still carried their cap-'n'-ball revolvers then. But not Mr. Tyrell. He had a conversion made on his Army Colt so that it shot them new *metallic* cartridges—mighty interesting, if you ask me."

"What about their daughter, Valerie?"

"That Indian girl is a story in herself, but her past is pretty much a mystery to most folks. The Kincades adopted the girl shortly before the war. Raised her like she was white. All the rest is pure speculation." He finished the shave and said, "That'll be two bits for the shave and bath, mister."

Langely paid him, and as he started for the door, he heard the barber clucking behind him. "Looky there. Ain't yet seven thirty and those boys are already gathering in front of the Silver Lady. Appears it's going to be another one of them days."

Outside, Langely eyed the knot of men loitering in front of the saloon. He stifled a grin as he untied his horse. Leading the animal across the street, Langely watched them out of the corner of his eye. As he suspected they would, they left the shade beneath the wide porch and came out into the street.

A fellow in dusty clothes who smelled like he needed a bath worse than Langely had, walked a broad circle around Langely in the middle of the street. The man's mouth turned down in a frown, and he said, "He don't look like no Chinaman. I thought you said he was yellow, Jake?"

The one who answered to the name laughed. He planted his fist on his hips and shook his head. "I didn't mean he was yellow on the outside. I meant he was yellow on the inside!"

"That right, mister? Are you yellow on the inside?"

There were five of them. A slouched and tattered bunch in desperate need of the services of the bathhouse Langely had just left. Their broad hats protected bloodshot eyes from the morning sun. They had drunk too much whiskey the night before and slept too few hours. They all wore revolvers, but Langely didn't think they planned on using them in broad daylight. That would be too much like murder. It was going to be fists, not guns, and they were well prepared for that kind of fight.

"You boys sure you have the right fellow?" Langely said easily, yet as he spoke, muscles tightened beneath his shirt, ready.

"I think so," the first man said. "You're that no-account that busted up Hank's game last night. You weren't wearing a gun then and you ain't wearing one now. That sort of proves you're a yellow coward, don't it, boys?"

They all seemed to agree on this.

"Any man lets himself be called a coward and don't do anything about it must be one," another said.

The fellow standing closest to Langely glanced at the ground, as if distracted, and then without warning wheeled about with bunched fists. His knuckles found only empty air as Langely ducked beneath them and came up with a staggering blow that sent the man reeling back, buckled over into the street. Then suddenly they were all over him.

Langely fought free of their arms and felt a jaw crunch beneath his fist. The three remaining came at him as a single man. One of them connected, and Langely spun away, with the street rushing up to meet him. Instantly back on his feet, he parried a flying set of knuckles and brought his toe up into an exposed groin, promptly putting down a third contender. He turned his attention on the remaining two antagonists, who seemed to hesitate now, as if waiting. Then someone grabbed him from behind and pinned his arms.

"Got him, Al?" the one called Jake asked.

"Got him," answered a man Langely could not see. Langely arched his back against this new rival. A fist swept out. Langely rolled with the blow and braced himself for the next when a pistol fired and Burt Jenney's voice came from behind him. "Break it up! Break it up now, or I'll throw the lot of you in jail!"

Jenney marched into view. The gent at Langely's front eyed the revolver in the sheriff's hand and relaxed out of his fisticuff stance. He unclenched his hand and picked his hat off the street. "We was just having a little fun, sheriff," he said.

The man behind Langely let go of his arms. Slowly

the three sprawled in the street picked themselves up and stumbled away.

Burt watched the last of them file into the saloon before holstering the revolver. "For a man fresh in town, Mr. Bracken, you have a habit of making enemies of the wrong kind of men."

"Trouble is the last thing I'm after, sheriff." He recovered his hat, pushed his fingers through his hair, and pulled it down over his head.

Jenney gave a short laugh. "I believe you, mister, a man like you who doesn't wear a gun." He paused. "Maybe if you started carrying it again, folks wouldn't be so eager to make trouble. Not wearing a gun just naturally makes you a target for certain types we have around here. They consider it downright unmanly." He smiled. "Don't give me that surprised, I-don't-know-what-you're-talking-about look, Mr. Bracken. You can fool most people, but you can't fool me. I've been standing behind this badge too many years not to recognize the type. I'd say you're a man accustomed to carrying a gun, and my gut feeling tells me you're a man that knows how to use one."

Langely gathered up the reins to his horse. "What makes you think so?"

"Signs, mister, signs," Jenney said. "They're written all over you."

"What kind of signs might they be?"

"It's like when a man comes into town. You know right off he's a city boy by his boots." They started walking toward the café. "You see, a dude will not have spur marks on his heels." Jenney lifted his left foot and displayed the gouges in the leather on his heel. "That's the kind of signs I mean.

"As for you, well, your signs are of a different nature. I noticed a couple of things right off. The way you hold your right arm when you're walking and not thinking about it—sort of cocked and ready. And your pants. They are all faded from the sun except the back of your legs. That tells me you spend a lot of hours in the saddle. And then there's that patch on your right hip, not quite as faded as the rest of your britches. It is just about the size of a holster. It ain't too big of a patch, so I guess you carry a short-barreled Colt." He smiled. "They are all signs, boy, if you've got an eye to read 'em.

"Well, it ain't none of my business, and I'm not one to pry. A man's life is his own private affair so long as he doesn't make trouble in my town." Jenney narrowed an eye at him. "So long as he don't make trouble for me, I won't cause him any. You have a good day, now, Mr. Bracken, and try to stay out of the Double T's way." The sheriff ambled away down the sidewalk.

Langely tied his horse in front of the La Casa Luna, adding Burt Jenney to his growing list of people to watch.

The café was busier than it had been the evening before, and he had to take a table along the window, feeling uneasy without a wall to turn his back to. Another one of those changes he'd have to get used to, he told himself. He ordered breakfast when the Mexican woman came around, and as he waited for the bacon and eggs, sipping the coffee she had left, he tried to make some order out of the events of the last twelve hours.

Out the window he watched Burt Jenney come up the opposite side of the street. Jenney paused in front of the bank, looked up and down the length of the street, and stepped into the alleyway. When he was in the shadows, he skipped up the flight of steps to the second floor of the bank and rapped on the door. In a moment it opened, and he disappeared inside.

The Mexican woman came with his food then.

"Who lives above the bank?" he asked her.

"Above the bank, señor?" she asked. "The banker, Señor Caldwell. 'E likes to sleep on top of all 'is money!" She laughed and left, shaking her head.

9

"Silk! Real silk! Oh, Sarah, it's lovely—when did you get it?" Valerie Kincade said, caressing the material between her fingers. "I never expected to see anything this fine in Esteros Creek. My word, just the feel of it takes me back to New York."

Sarah looked up from the cash drawer, where she was counting out the morning's change. "This may be the middle of the New Mexico Territory, but that doesn't mean we have to be uncivilized."

"Oh, I didn't mean . . ."

"I know what you meant, Val." Sarah closed the drawer and took down a second bolt of silk from the shelf.

"Since Dad died, I've begun to stock a lot of items he never would have dreamed of carrying. You know how Dad was. A businessman through and through. As practical and old-fashioned as rain. 'Sturdy shoes and gabardine!'—that's what Dad used to say. 'In this country you dress for the land!' . . . well, that's what he used to say."

Sarah's voice became distant. She shrugged her shoulders and touched the smooth material. "I don't know if it will ever sell in Esteros Creek. I never did have Dad's business sense, but a woman needs a touch of elegance now and then."

"Oh, I agree, Sarah." Valerie pulled an end of the silk against herself and bunched it around her narrow waist. "How does it look?"

"Beautiful, Val. Like it was woven for a princess."

"A princess?" Valerie laughed. "Mother always said my great-grandfather was a chief. That almost makes me a princess. Sarah, do you think it would be too flashy?"

"Too flashy? You mean for your party dress?"

"Yes. . . ."

"It would make a lovely dress!"

"Then I'll buy it! I can start sewing as soon as I get home this afternoon."

"You'll be the envy of the town—"

"Lace. The dress will need lace, soft and delicate."

"I have some in back."

"Sarah, this makes me want to run right back to New York. New York City has stores that sell nothing but lace; yards and yards and yards of delicate, exquisite lace, imported from England and Spain. And silk too! Shelves of silk!" Valerie paused breathlessly.

"You ought to see the dresses women are wearing back east. They feel almost alive. They flow with you when you walk, not like this old cotton thing that just hangs and gets in the way."

"It's different out here," Sarah said.

"I know." Valerie fell back on the stool and sighed, still clutching the silk to herself. "I sometimes wish Mother had never sent me away to school. I would never have known what I was missing if I'd stayed on the ranch." She looked up. "It's more than fine clothes and cobblestone streets, you know. It's the people. They're different."

"Different?"

"Never mind. I'm rattling on like a spoiled school-girl."

Sarah said, "I've never told you this, but all my life I've envied you living in a big house, surrounded by servants and dashing young cowboys. I just knew that what you had was all a body needed to be happy, and sometimes I wished it was me instead of you." She gave a short laugh. "I guess it takes more than a fancy house and money to make a person happy." Her voice turned serious. "Why did you come back?"

Valerie's ebony eyes lifted, and for a moment the two girls looked at each other. During her years growing up in Esteros Creek, Sarah Lawrence had been her only real friend. They were so different and yet, in some ways, so alike.

"Life in the West isn't easy, but it's harder than you can imagine if God made you an Indian. Mother is old now, and unfriendly times are on her. The Kincades took me in at a time when most white folks would have thrown an orphaned Indian baby to the wolves. They raised me as their own, helped me through the hard times, saw to it I received an education—a good education! Now Father is dead and Mother has no one but me. I owe it to her, Sarah. No! Not 'owe'—I *want* to

help. Just as they helped me. That's why I came back."
Valerie stood off the stool. "Now will you look at me."
Her voice lost its somberness and she smiled. "I'm talking myself into a state of pure melancholy when, after all, I really have so much to be thankful for. I have a friend like you, I have Mother, I have the ranch, and there's that nice Mr. Bracken to drive Joe and me home today. Why should I be gloomy? . . . Sarah, is something wrong? You're looking queerly."

"No, of course not," she said quickly, "what could be wrong? I better go back and find that lace you wanted, Val, I won't be a minute—"

Sarah was stopped by the opening of the front door. Louis Easterman tucked his walking stick under his arm and came across the room in brisk strides. He smiled and bowed curtly at the two women.

"Miss Lawrence, how are you this fine morning?" he asked, tipping his derby hat off his head.

"I'm fine, thank you, Mr. Easterman."

Easterman turned to Valerie, his green eyes bright and friendly. "And Miss Kincade. What a pleasure to see you once more. I heard you were back from school. I must say, the east hasn't hurt you one bit!"

"Why, thank you, Mr. Easterman. I just returned last week. You're looking well yourself."

"I can't complain. I've expanded my law firm, you know. Took on a bright young attorney from Denver—a nice lad, I'll have to introduce you. Lately I've been doing a little speculating in real estate and, well, that's why I stopped by." He turned back to Sarah. "Have you considered my offer, Miss Lawrence?"

"Your offer is quite generous, Mr. Easterman, but I'm really not ready to sell the store."

Louis Easterman surveyed the store with a critical eye, balancing his weight on the narrow stick. After a moment he returned his gaze to Sarah. "Is business doing well?"

"Well enough."

"It is a large store. . . ."

"I am managing the business quite satisfactorily, thank you," she said, irritated.

Louis Easterman smiled. "Well, in that case I wish you all the best—but remember, if you decide to sell, I'll make you the best offer in town!"

"He's really a very nice man, Sarah," Valerie said after Easterman had gone.

Sarah frowned. "I just get tired of people feeling sorry for this *poor little lady with the big store*! I can handle it. I've done so almost a year now. Why don't they leave me alone." Sarah paused then shrugged her shoulders. "I almost forgot, I was going to find that lace you wanted. I'll be right back." She disappeared through the back door.

A moment later Thomas Langely came in the front door.

"Good morning, Mr. Bracken," Valerie said as he stepped out of the harsh morning light and removed his hat. When he gazed down at her, she wished she had known to bring along another dress. This blue one was starting to show the strain of a long day and night.

"Good morning, Miss Kincade. I trust you're feeling better?"

"Much better, thank you. Sarah and I went to bed shortly after you left; however, Joe and Mr. Lemont"— she shook her head—"they must have gotten another bottle from somewhere. We heard them carrying on and telling tales half the night. I swear, I don't know where men get the stamina for such things."

"Some men." He grinned and nodded out the front window. "I see the boy brought your carriage by."

"Yes, he came about twenty minutes ago. We've been waiting."

"I had a few things to see to."

Sarah came from the back room then. Valerie was surprised when Sarah's face turned to flint.

"Good morning, Miss Lawrence," Langely said. "That's a striking dress you have on."

Sarah looked down at herself and wrinkled her nose. "Why, this old thing! I declare, it's about ready for the rag bag." Her eyebrows contracted into a scowl. "I see you finally showed up. We've been waiting on you." She turned to Valerie. "This is all the lace I have. I hope it will be enough."

"That will be fine," Valerie said, dismayed at Sarah's abruptness.

How many yards of that silk did you need?" Sarah seemed unable to keep the sharp note of impatience from her voice.

"I'm not sure." Valerie glanced at Langely. "Will you excuse us?"

The women moved off to the counter. "How is Joe?" he asked in a voice loud enough for the man in the back room to hear.

A croaking reply came from beyond the doorway. "Joe is still alive . . . barely."

Langely grinned and left the ladies chatting by the counter. He found Joe Lascoe sitting on the edge of the cot, his elbows on his knees, a drawn and weary face cradled in his hands.

"You look terrible," he noted cheerfully.

Joe groaned and lifted his head off his palms. "And that's just how I feel. My head's a throbbing like a herd of them Texican longhorns stampeded all over it. And these bandages! I'm all tied up and I got me an itch where I can't reach to scratch!"

Langely pulled a chair around, straddling it. "I hear you and Lemont got oiled up last night."

Joe narrowed an eye. "It were civilized booze. No behind-the-barn brew, that stuff." He leaned forward and lowered his voice. "That Lemont is a bad influence! The man has bottles hid in the most unusual places—reckon newspaper work does that to a man?"

Langely laughed and shrugged his shoulders. "I couldn't say."

"You watch yourself he ever invites you to share a bottle! Oooowww, Lord, it hurts to stand."

"Let me give you a hand." He helped Joe off the cot and walked him through the door out into the store. Sarah was wrapping the silk. She handed the brown paper bundle to Valerie and said, "You two be careful and have a safe ride. Joe, don't be forgetting you're sixty-one years old with a couple of broken ribs that need mending." Sarah narrowed a critical eye at Langely. "I hope you can take care of Valerie and Joe if trouble comes up."

She was a high-spirited girl, and he liked that, but he detected a hint of something else in her stinging comment, which he tried to ignore. "If we happen to run into trouble, Joe has his six-gun, and the way Miss Kincade handles a Winchester, I don't think we need to worry about highwaymen."

He helped Joe outside and onto the floorboards in the rear of the carriage and offered a hand to Valerie as she stepped up to the seat. He tied his horse behind and climbed up beside her, turning the carriage around in the street. Valerie waved good-bye to Sarah, then fastened her sunbonnet securely about her chin, smoothed her dress, and looked back at Joe lying on the blankets. "You let us know if the ride gets too rough, Joe."

"Yes, ma'am. It can't be any rougher than that fellow's fists last night."

Above the bank a curtain parted as the carriage moved up the street. The curtain dropped back in place, and the man behind it, Martin Caldwell, frowned as he crossed a small carpeted living room. He struck a match and put it to the tip of a fat cigar. "Think this fellow, Bracken, can cause us any trouble?" he said around the cigar.

Burt Jenney pulled the cup of coffee away from his lips and shook his head. "I don't know, Martin. I just don't know. It's an unfortunate time for a stranger to drift into town and get chummy with the Kincades. In another month it wouldn't have made any difference, but now—?" Jenney shrugged his shoulders.

"You are certain he is not what he claims to be?"

"A shopkeeper? Part truth, maybe. But the man is hiding something. I don't know what it is yet, but I'll find out. I checked my files and old posters and didn't come up with a thing. Yet I've got a deep-down gut feeling, and I've been a lawman too many years to ignore it."

Martin Caldwell snatched the cigar from his mouth and poked it at Jenney. "You keep an eye on him. We've worked too long and too hard to let this deal slip through our fingers. We both have too much to lose. Remember what's riding on this and don't let anyone get in our way and mess it up, hear?"

Jenney came out of the chair. "Don't lecture me, Caldwell." His eyes hardened. "I know what's coming down as well as you, and I'm not about to let anyone spoil it, not now."

Caldwell bit down on his cigar and studied Jenney. "Okay, Burt, okay. This Bracken fellow has made me jumpy." He turned back to the window and parted the curtains again. "The town's coming awake. I better get downstairs and open up the bank."

Burt Jenney retrieved his hat from the table. "We'll talk later." He poked his head outside the door to check the alley, then turned back. "Stop worrying about Bracken. You just make sure everything is tied up nice and legal on your end. I'll take care of the Kincades—and that stranger if he causes us any trouble."

The sheriff left then, but he paused on the landing of the stairs to glance back through the small side window at Martin Caldwell, who was watching the street from the front window again. Then Caldwell ground the cigar in an ashtray and reached for his hat.

Burt Jenney hurried down the steps and across the street and into the jailhouse.

10

Thomas Langely let his eyes sweep across the broad expanse of sere grass growing hot under the morning sun. He looked at the dark-haired woman sitting silently at his side. "It's a fine morning, isn't it, Miss Kincade?" he said in an attempt to break the silence that ensued since they had left Esteros Creek, and Sarah Lawrence, behind. A silence not of any ill feelings, but rather of two people who didn't know each other very well. The weather was always a good place to start. Nobody ever got very emotional over the weather.

Valerie smiled at him and shaded her eyes against the low morning sun. "They are all pretty, Mr. Bracken. In New Mexico the mornings are always beautiful."

Tawny grass rolled gently in the wind like waves on a vast brown sea. He said, "From the looks of it I'd say this land is thick with quail. There isn't anything I like better than to hunt quail, ma'am. Give me a shotgun and a bird dog with a soft mouth. Set me loose in quail country and you might never see me again."

Valerie laughed. "You would have liked my father. He was a bird hunter too. I remember early mornings with the frost still white on the grass. We'd start hunting with the sun just coming up, and by eight o'clock we'd have more birds than I could carry. Mother used to have fits—hunting wasn't a girls' sport, you see. It wasn't proper for her little girl to put on a pair of britches and shoulder a shotgun. But you never met anyone as bull-headed as Father. Mother didn't have a chance."

Langely grinned. "This is real pleasant country. Plenty of grass, plenty of water. Good range."

"At one time we ran fifty thousand head," Valerie said proudly. "The herd at times stretched from one horizon to the other and then some. Folks used to say they'd never seen anything like it since the days of the buffalo. I was a little girl when buffalo were here. I don't remember too much of it now, but I do remember the cattle."

"That would be quite a sight, Miss Kincade." Langely wasn't so young that he couldn't remember the vast seas of bison drifting for days past his parents' cabin along the Bitter Creek in Wyoming.

"Yes, quite a sight," Valerie agreed, but the short laugh she gave was acrid. "But not a legacy a girl would relish, Mr. Bracken. I was riding horses before I was walking. Shooting guns while most girls played with dolls. I spent my days alone, playing make-believe. You don't find many children your age to play with in the middle of a half-million acres."

Langely kept his eyes on the road ahead. "I guess I

look at it the way a man sees it." He gave the reins a flick. "I don't see them the way a lady would."

"I shouldn't be snippy, Mr. Bracken—"

"Thomas," he interrupted, smiling.

Valerie flushed. "Thomas," she corrected. "It's just that I've had a taste of something different. I'm no longer satisfied with what the Largo or Esteros Creek can offer."

"You mean the East?"

She nodded her head. "It tends to stick with you even after you leave. I haven't been able to shake it loose. Of course I've only been back home a week, but I don't think I'll ever have the same feeling for this place as when I left. It's not the land, or even the ranch, it's . . ." She hesitated, then looked hard into his eyes. "I don't want to sound superior, but frankly I don't like the people."

She went on quickly, as if to defend her position. "In the East people accept me for what I am. Most people don't even know I'm an *Indian*." She pronounced the word with disdain. "New York is a city full of people who have never seen an Indian. To them I'm Valerie Kincade, a rancher's daughter from a far-off place called New Mexico, and if my skin happens to be a shade darker than theirs, it's because I grew up in the West, where the sun shines three hundred days a year— or at least that's what they think."

She folded her nut-brown arms and gazed out across the dry grass. A rush of color tinted her neck and cheeks.

Langely returned his eyes to the road. He couldn't deny that the world was full of injustice, but that all western people were hostile toward Indians and all eastern folks Indian-tolerant was an idea he found hard to swallow. Similar notions had made him pull up roots in Montana and ride south a thousand miles, only to learn that people were the same wherever you went.

Langely glanced back at Joe Lascoe. The old man had managed to fall asleep in the cramped space behind their seats.

Valerie said, "I'm sorry I vented my frustrations on you, Mr. Bracken." Her eyes avoided his as she scratched at an imagined speck on her blue dress. "Life hasn't been all that bad for me, not like it has for some folks."

"I understand, Miss Kincade."

"Please, call me Valerie, Mr. . . ." she hesitated and then smiled. "I mean, Thomas."

"Valerie it is." He nodded up the road. "What's ahead between here and the Largo?" The question expertly changed the subject, but that wasn't his reason for asking. Like Joe's itch that he couldn't quite reach to scratch, his concerns kept coming back to those five riders he watched leave town by the north road.

She shrugged her shoulders. "Practically nothing. About a mile east of here is the old Porter place, but it's abandoned now. Other than that, just a lot of grass, and of course the cottonwood forest down where the road crosses the Old River."

"Cottonwood forest?"

"It's just about the largest stand of cottonwood trees within a hundred miles. It crosses the southern edge of the ranch," she said, amused that he knew nothing of what must have been a venerable regional landmark. "Folks were calling it a forest as long as I can remember. Of course most folks in these parts have never seen more than twelve trees together at one time." She laughed, "I used to think it was a forest, too, until I went back east and saw what a real forest looks like. This road cuts right through the middle of it and crosses the Old River—actually it's named the Porter River, and it used to carry a lot of water before Father built a dam across a canyon many years ago. Now only a trickle of water flows, that's why we call it the *Old River*."

"I've seen oak-tree forests and birch-tree forests and pine-tree forests, but I cannot recall ever seeing any cottonwood-tree forests." He smiled and quickened the horses' pace with an easy flick of the reins, but his mind was racing ahead. He glanced down at the Winchester on the floor, then back at Joe Lascoe, asleep on the blankets. The old man's holster belt was folded and tossed in a corner.

"If it's a cottonwood-tree forest you want to see, Thomas, then at the top of that next hill stop and look down along the bottom of the valley."

"That close?" He edged his words with surprise, to hide the concern that was suddenly upon him.

She nodded her head. "And north of the stream, as far as you can see, is all Largo land!" Her eyes were smiling, her words boastful.

Well, why not! If it were his half-million acres, he'd be boasting too.

11

Brad Manning glanced up from the cards he was shuffling and grinned at the man hunched forward a few yards away where sunlight through the tree tops dappled the ground. "You should be more careful with that thing, Lowe," he said. Across from Manning, sitting cross-legged on the ground, Will Tanner chuckled, and Archie Duncan hid a grin behind his fist.

Lowe's eyes narrowed darkly. "Mind your own business."

Manning gave an easy, unshakable shrug. "I once had a friend who practiced pulling the gun from the holster —like you. He became a pretty fast hand until the day he put a bullet through his leg, right here above the knee. It came out down by his ankle." Manning shook his head. "The doctor had to cut the whole leg clean off." Manning tapped his thigh, then as an afterthought added, "My friend died."

Tanner laughed. "Stop talking, Brad, and start dealing. You don't want to make Sidney nervous."

Lowe scowled, shoved the revolver into his holster, and scuffed through the dried leaves up a short incline from the river to the road where Hank Acker was leaning against a tree, putting a match to a cigar.

"What happened back there?" Acker asked through a haze of blue smoke.

"Manning's acting like a mother hen again. Any sign of 'em yet?"

"Ain't seen a thing. Got Harve up that tree for a lookout, but it wouldn't surprise me if they spent the whole day in town while we sit out here on our butts waiting."

"Give them another hour, then we'll go looking." Lowe nudged Hank in the arm. "Hey, if it was me knowing what I was going to have all to myself, I'd be singing like a lark. What's bothering you, Acker?"

Yesterday night, with his brain wading in eighty-proof whiskey and the sting of the Indian girl backing him down still fresh in his mind, the idea sounded good. Now he wasn't so sure. They were six men going up against a girl and an old man. The thought irked him.

"Nothing's bothering me. Nothing." Acker pushed away from the tree and shuffled up the hill where Will Tanner, Brad Manning, and Archie Duncan were playing poker.

"Deal you in next hand?" Brad asked when Acker hunkered down beside them.

"Sure."

"What's happening, Hank?"

"Not much."

"If you was to ask me, Hank," Brad said, "I'd say we

forget the girl and stay right here under this big shady tree and play poker all day long."

"That's because you're winning," Will Tanner said irritably. "If they don't come pretty soon, Hank, I'm riding back to town while I still have some money left—before I lose it all to this cardsharp."

Brad laughed. "How long you going to hang around here, Hank?"

"I don't know. Another hour maybe."

Brad said, "You know, if old man Tyrell finds out about this, it won't sit well with him."

Hank frowned and nodded his head. "I've been pondering that."

"The Tyrells look with favor on you, Hank. Sooner or later Jeff is going to take over the old man's holdings, and when he does, he's going to be needing a new foreman. The job might fall your way if you play your cards right."

"What are you trying to say?"

"The Kincades and the Tyrells, they go back a long way together," Brad went on easily. "Everyone knows how Tyrell feels about Old Lady Kincade, but he might feel differently about the girl. He ain't got no quarrel with her, as far as I know. Maybe Tyrell feels something special toward her." Brad shrugged his shoulders. "I'm not saying he does. It's just something to think about."

"I have been," Hank said.

Then Harve Winter yelled down from his perch up the tree. "Hank! I see them! They're stopped on top of the next rise. They're just sitting there, only two of 'em —like you figured."

Sidney Lowe scuffed hurriedly beneath the trees.

"Good, good," he said with bald eagerness. "Get down out of that tree, Harve. Everyone, out of sight!"

Despite his doubts Acker found himself drawn to Lowe's enthusiasm.

Albert Canon wobbled like a winding-down top, staggering from storefront to balcony pillar like a bronc-thrown cowboy and guzzling whiskey as he went. After the failed attack on Langely that morning, he and the others had retreated to the Silver Lady Saloon. He had been tipping down the last of his first bottle when the message came that Burt Jenney wanted to see him. A second bottle procured for the journey, Canon told his friends he'd be back later and stumbled out into the aching sunlight, shielding his eyes with a hand. Cursing the morning, he had propelled himself in the general direction of Burt Jenney's office.

On the sidewalk in front of Sarah Lawrence's store, his uncertain progress halted, and with a shoulder braced against the painted windowpanes, he tipped up the bottle.

A movement inside drew his attention, and he squinted through the window. Sarah had stepped up on a short ladder and was stretching for a box on a top shelf. The motion raised her skirt enough to show the smooth curve of her calf, and for a fleeting moment Al's eyes caressed the graceful, stockinged leg.

It wasn't as if Albert Canon had never seen a woman's leg before. The girls at the saloon were always revealing their legs in a casual, practiced sort of way. Good for a drink, and perhaps an indulgence of another kind later on. But they were just bar girls; that was their job. Sarah Lawrence, on the other hand, was a respectable lady. What she had couldn't be bought for two dollars and a bottle of whiskey. That made it infinitely more desirable.

His heartbeat quickened, his body tingled as his imagination delved deeper and deeper into the forbidden mysteries that lay hidden above Sarah's shapely leg. The thought overwhelmed him, and he forgot Jenney's summons.

"Canon!" Jenney barked from the doorway of the sheriff's office next door.

"Huh?" Canon wheeled at the sound of his name, and recalled his original destination.

"You're drunk again, Canon. Get in here!"

Canon reeled away from the entrance. *Later,* he promised himself, *I'll see to her later.*

The darkness inside Jenney's office eased the throbbing behind his eyes some, and Canon fell into a chair and tipped the bottle up again.

Jenney snatched it away.

"What the—?"

"It's not yet nine o'clock in the morning and you are already stone drunk!"

Canon grinned stupidly and turned up his palms in a what-do-you-expect gesture.

Jenney shut the door. The office darkened as he pulled down the shades. To a man just in from the bright sunlight it was black as the belly of a cave. Canon rubbed his eyes. Suddenly Jenney was standing over him. He yanked Canon from the chair and propelled him across the room and against the back wall, rattling the rifles in the rack there. Canon's eyes expanded as Jenney grabbed up a handful of his sweaty shirt.

"I told you I didn't want to see you anywhere near that stranger."

Canon tried to speak, but Jenney jerked him away from the wall and sent him sprawling across the floor. His nose smashed on the rough floorboards, and blood spilled to the dirty wooden planks. Canon rolled to his back. Jenney planted a foot on the squirming man's chest.

"When I pay a man, I expect him to follow my orders! Do I make myself clear?"

Canon sputtered, and nodded his head.

"Try remembering that the next time you decide to take matters into your own hands." Jenney nudged him in the side with the toe of his boot. "Now, get up."

Canon grappled for the chair, cowered into it, and dabbed his nose with his shirtsleeve. Jenney pulled back a corner of the shade to peer out into the street. After a moment he turned and considered the quaking man in the chair. "There's water and a towel in back. Clean yourself up, and then I'll tell you what I want Hank and the boys to do tonight."

"What's wrong, Thomas?"

Langely frowned as his gray eyes swept across the grove of cottonwood trees ahead. The horses stood alert, their ears cocked forward. Maybe he was making too much of what he had seen earlier. He looked at Valerie. "I don't know. Just a feeling."

She followed his gaze up the road that lay dark beneath the spreading trees and seemed suddenly to understand. "You don't think . . . last night?"

Minutes earlier, from the ridge where Valerie had asked him to stop, he had carefully examined the distant trees that swelled around the road and sprawled along the shallow riverbed. It was indeed a forest, judging by its length and breadth. From the high vantage point Langely had seen nothing, but half a dozen men and horses could easily escape detection under that thick cover, especially if escaping detection was their intent.

He gave Valerie a look that answered her question.

"Those men were drunk. They've probably forgotten all about it by now!" Her eyebrows drew together, her lips compressed. "You don't really think . . . ?" She left the question unfinished.

He could think of no good reason to tell her about the six riders that rode out of town that morning, or of the fight in front of the barbershop. There was no sense alarming her if he was wrong, and if he wasn't, she would find out for herself soon enough.

"I'm afraid I don't have your faith in human nature, but if I'm wrong—and I hope I am—I will be happy to apologize on the other side. Meanwhile hold on."

He gave a shout and cracked the whip above the team. The startled horses reared, and the carriage lurched forward with a creak of its leather riggings. Valerie rocked back into the seat, clutched the armrest with one hand, and secured the bonnet to the top of her head with the other. Joe slid against the rear of the carriage and came awake with a groan.

"What the devil!" he bellowed. "What's going on? Miss Kincade . . . ?"

The horses pulled ahead and moved into a full gallop. Valerie called back. "Mr. Bracken is protecting us from unseen dangers, Joe. Just hold tight. As soon as we are through the forest, he promises to drive more sanely."

Joe grabbed the rear of the seat and hoisted himself up. "You expectin' trouble, Thomas?"

"I'm just scratching an itch, Joe." He cracked the whip above the horses again, and then the cottonwoods were on either side of the road and closing in behind.

Valerie turned an amused eye on him and tightened her grasp on the seat.

Her amusement was short-lived.

In the roadway ahead two men had jumped out from the shadows of the trees, and they were drawing their revolvers as the carriage rushed toward them.

Acker and Lowe watched the team loom larger until at the very last moment they leaped aside, and the carriage swept between them.

Lowe rolled off the shoulder of the road and sprang to his feet watching the cloud of dust churning toward the river and Valerie Kincade's wide-eyed face staring back at him.

Acker stepped out into the road, brushing himself off. "That stranger was driving! Did you see?" he said, excited.

"I saw," Lowe said, finding his hat and tugging it onto his head. Will Tanner brought their horses from the trees. They leaped into their saddles and buried their heels.

12

"They're following us," she said urgently.

"I'm not at all surprised."

"You knew! You knew they'd be waiting for us." Valerie's eyes narrowed suspiciously. "But how could you . . . ?"

Langely cracked the whip above the team. "Your Winchester is on the floor, Miss Kincade. Don't use it unless they start shooting first, then, when you do, be careful of my horse tied back there."

She reached for the rifle. Rushing wind caught the frilly little hat and tore it from her head. Long black hair streamed back.

"Damn!"

Langely turned an amused eye at her as she grappled for the rifle from under the seat.

The carriage clattered through the shallow water and up the far bank. Valerie levered a shell into the Winchester and looked back through the cloud of gray dust churning up behind them.

"They're gaining!"

He ventured a quick glance over his shoulder. Joe Lascoe was fumbling his pistol from the holster and trying to brace himself against the side of the rocking carriage.

"Remember," Langely said turning back to the road, "no shooting unless they start it!"

The road curved sharply, and the narrow, steel-rimmed wheels skipped across the mud-dried ruts. Langely fought the reins through the curve, and as the carriage firmed up when the road straightened, he used the whip again.

Langely cursed beneath his breath when the first bullet whined through the air somewhere close. He had hoped to avoid gunfire, but now that was beyond his control. He turned to Joe and said, "Cut my horse loose!"

Joe untied the halter lead, and the horse veered off the road, galloping alongside a short distance, then out into the tall grass.

Valerie shouldered her rifle and struggled to steady its jittery sights on the oncoming riders.

"Remember that Joe is back there."

She glared at him, coal-black eyes shining. "I'm not in the habit of shooting hired hands or horses, Mr. Bracken!" she said hotly, wheeling away and squinting down the barrel of her rifle.

The Winchester barked. She levered in a fresh shell. Behind him came the sharp report of Joe's pistol. He put his two passengers out of mind and concentrated on working the team. The carriage lurched, gaining speed now that his horse was no longer holding it back, and he used the whip again.

Dave Thompson brought his horse to a stop and raised a hand for the others to draw up—a habit he couldn't quite shed as easily as he had shed his army blues after the war. The riders slowed their mounts and halted beside him. Dave cocked his head, listening to the faint wind.

"Why we stopping, Dave?" Bill Tremely asked.

"Gunshots," Dave said, scanning the crest of a distant rise.

"I didn't hear anything." Bill looked at the other men.

Edgar squinted at the rise. "Yeah, I can hear 'em now. Real faint—far off."

Dave said, "Two or three pistols, and at least one rifle —coming from the river."

"Miss Kincade—?" Theodore Tremely asked, and glanced from his brother, Bill, to Dave.

Dave Thompson shook his head. "Can't be sure, but that rifle sounds a lot like her Pa's old 'seventy-three. Let's find out." He kicked his horse ahead, and the riders from the Largo Ranch fell in behind.

Langely knew they could not hold their lead. He looked over at Valerie Kincade, who was having trouble aiming the rifle while keeping her long hair from fluttering into her eyes. Joe Lascoe poured out lead as quickly as it came in, but the swaying carriage was no place to aim a gun from.

"How far to the ranch?" he yelled above the roar of the steel-rimmed wheels and pounding horses.

Valerie squeezed off another shot and cried, "I'm out of bullets, Thomas!"

"How far!" he shouted again.

"What?"

"The Largo! . . . How far are we?"

She pulled a tangle of hair from her eyes and winced as a bullet creased the air near her head. "It's eleven miles from the river."

He shook his head. "We can't keep ahead of them that long! I'm going to stop the team over the next rise. We'll use the carriage for cover. It's the only chance we have."

"Thomas, I'm out of bullets! We haven't anything to fight with!"

Langely looked back at Joe. "How you fixed for bullets, Joe?"

"I've got maybe six, seven left, Thomas!"

That left him no choice but to continue the race as long as he could. He used the whip and felt the horses straining at their harnesses. A bullet tore splinters from the seat between them; another hissed near his ear. The carriage rumbled over the crest of the next hill and down the far side. For a brief moment the ridge top protected their backs.

Then Valerie clutched his arm and pointed up the road. "Look!" she exclaimed. Ahead was the dust of riders approaching fast.

Langely glanced over his shoulder. Their pursuers had seen the oncoming riders, too, and had reined to a stop at the top of the ridge, watching the carriage flee. Langely played in the reins, easing the frantic horses to a stop. They rolled past the Largo men, who opened an alley for the slowing carriage and circled behind as it came to a halt.

Dave Thompson reined in alongside them. "Are you all right, Miss Kincade?" he said, but he was looking at Langely. He was a big man, and he rode a horse to match his size. His face was old leather, his brown eyes harsh and wary of strangers. It was an ageless face. It could have belonged to a man of forty or sixty—after a certain number of years a face baked by the sun doesn't change much.

"We're fine Dave . . . now."

Thompson studied Langely.

"This is Mr. Bracken," Valerie said. "He helped us in town. We had some trouble with the Double T again."

"Your mama was afraid that might be the case." He nodded toward the ridge. "That them we saw turn back?"

"Yes."

His eyes shifted to the rear of the carriage. "What's wrong with Joe?"

"He got himself into a fight with some of the Double T boys," Valerie said, "Thomas . . . er, Mr. Bracken helped stop it."

Dave's face widened into a smile. "It's okay, Joe, you can stop hiding your head now. The shooting is all over."

When Joe didn't move, the smile slipped from Dave's lips. "Joe . . . ?"

Langely leaped over the seat as Thompson swung off his horse and came around the back. He rolled Joe to his back and felt warm moistness on his fingers. A red stain was spreading across the front of his shirt. "He's dead."

"No!" Valerie cried.

Langely laid Joe back down.

Valerie found a handkerchief somewhere in a bag and put it to her eyes.

"Val—?" Dave started.

"I'll be all right," she said after a moment. "I'll be all right. Joe has been like a father to me ever since—"

"I know," Thompson said, and although his words were gentle, the harsh lines of his face remained, as if carved permanently in the leather skin. "I know, honey. Let's get you back to the house. Your ma is worrying herself sick over you." He said to Langely, "We'll follow along with the carriage, Mr. Bracken."

"My horse is running loose about a mile back."

"Billy, go round up Mr. Bracken's horse. If you see any of Tyrell's boys still around, come back and get us."

Billy swung his horse away and kicked it into motion.

Dave said to another man, "Larry, ride on ahead and tell Mrs. Kincade we found Valerie, and that she is unharmed. Say nothing about Joe if you can help it."

The rider started for the ranch in an easy lope.

Valerie looked back at Joe as Dave Thompson spread a blanket over him. Then she fixed her eye straight ahead and didn't look back again.

As he drove the team, Langely quietly cursed himself for not having done something to have prevented it. If he had brought his gun, maybe things would have turned out differently. Something inside him had warned him that those men would be waiting—he ignored the warning. He had had his chance at Hank Acker the night before—he had let the man live, and now Joe Lascoe was dead. He told himself it wasn't his fault. Somehow that didn't help.

* * *

A little before noon they looked down into a long valley, green with grass. The house, barns, and outbuildings were nestled among willow trees along a thin, sparkling thread of water. Langely guided the carriage off the ridge and under huge adobe portals where a wooden sign with the word LARGO carved in bold letters hung, weathered by sun and wind.

The carriage rolled to a stop in front of a rambling adobe house. An elderly woman came down the steps, holding tightly the peeled willow handrail. Valerie climbed off the carriage, and the old lady engulfed her in a long embrace. Dave swung down off his horse.

"I know what happened. Larry told me. Don't go blaming him, I know you told him not to, but I could see that something was wrong. It was written all over his face and in his voice."

Dave said, "I'll drive Joe into town this afternoon, then I'll pay Burt Jenney a visit." He turned to Bill Tremely. "Take the carriage to the bunkhouse.

"Wait." Martha Kincade went to the back of the carriage and lifted a corner of the blanket to look at Joe Lascoe's body. She whispered something too soft for Langely to hear, but he saw the tear that welled in her clear blue eyes a moment before she turned away and returned to her daughter's side.

Langely handed the reins over to the man who climbed into the seat, and the carriage pulled away. Valerie said, "Mother, this is Mr. Bracken. He helped Joe . . . us . . . yesterday in town."

Martha made an attempt at a smile. "Pleased to meet you, Mr. Bracken." Her hand was cold, yet her grasp strong, despite the drawn face and small shoulders that quivered now beneath the thin white blouse.

"I'm sorry about Joe."

Her lips drew tight. "So am I."

Bill Tremely came across the esplanade from the bunkhouse carrying a brown-paper bundle. "Miss Kincade, the package you left in the carriage. I'm afraid there is some blood on it, I hope it didn't ruin nothin'."

"Thank you, Billy—it doesn't matter."

"Let's get out of this sun," Martha said, turning back to the house.

Inside, a Mexican boy brought Langely a glass of water, and for a while nothing was said. Finally Valerie looked up. "What do we do now, Mother?"

"We'll let Burt handle it," she said. "We haven't had a killing on this ranch since your father died, and I'm not about to start up with Old Tyrell again—not as long as there is some other way."

Valerie frowned, started to speak, then glanced away. Martha said to Langely, "I want to thank you for the help you lent my daughter, and Joe. You're welcome to spend the night. The bunkhouse has more beds than we can fill these days."

"Thank you, Mrs. Kincade. But I'll be riding back to town with your men." He was suddenly thinking about Sarah Lawrence, and for a reason he did not understand, he wanted to be the one to tell her about Joe.

13

Acker and Lowe swung off their horses in front of the saloon and turned the reins around the hitching rail. Inside, Lowe ordered whiskey while Hank found Al Canon slumped across a table in the corner.

"Wake up, you no-account drunk," Acker said, pulling back a chair. Lowe came over carrying the drinks.

Canon raised his heavy head off his arms and rolled a bloodshot eye at the two men. He blinked, then pushed himself straight in the chair groaning. "Lord Almighty, I sure do need another whiskey." He eyed the glasses in their fingers.

Acker said, "That's the last thing you need. What happened to your face?"

Canon touched his swollen nose as if only vaguely aware of it and then lowered his head back to the table. Acker hauled him straight in the chair by his hair. "And what happened this morning?"

"Morning . . . ?" Canon mumbled.

"You were supposed to take care of that stranger. What went wrong?"

"Stranger . . . ?" Al's reddened eyelids widened. A pink web of blood vessels crisscrossed his eyeballs. "Oh, the stranger," he slurred, and groped for memories of the morning's events. "The sheriff . . . Burt . . . he broke it up."

"Jenney? You let Burt Jenney catch you? You're a fool, Canon!" Hank released the oily hair, and Canon slumped back to the table. They kicked back their chairs to leave, when Al mumbled something into his folded arms.

Acker turned back. "What?"

With great effort Al Canon pushed his head off the table and said, "Burt's got a job for you."

Hank leaned forward on his fists. "What kind of job?"

"He wants you to take a couple boys and some dynamite out to the Kincade place tonight and blow that dam at Porter Canyon." Al gave a crooked smile.

"The dam?" Hank swiveled an eye at Lowe. "Why?"

Canon shrugged a shoulder. "I don't know why. All's I know is that Burt, he don't want no one to get hurt or nothin'—just wants you to make sure that dam goes down."

"Why would he want us to blow the dam?" Acker said thoughtfully, glancing at Lowe.

"I said I didn't know." Canon's voice held a hint of irritation. "He didn't say. He just don't want nobody t' get hurt. He said it would complicate things."

"What else did Burt say?"

"That's all, Hank. That's all he told me." Canon laid

his head back onto his arms, and in a moment he was snoring.

"What do you make of that?"

"I don't know," Acker said.

"Looks like we got us a busy day ahead of us." Lowe had a gleeful anticipation in his eyes. "I always wanted to blow up a dam."

"Come on, let's get out of here," Acker said tossing down the last of his drink.

Burt Jenney lit his cigar in the flame of an oil lamp, leaned back, and blew a cloud of smoke at the ceiling. Across the room, hands clutched at his back, Martin Caldwell paced the floor. At the end of every other crossing, a single floorboard would squeak beneath the threadbare carpet as Caldwell turned on his heel and started back again. In the middle of one of these transits he stopped and looked up sharply.

"I don't like it, Jenney. I don't like it one bit!"

"Relax, Martin, everything has been taken care of." Burt eyed a fly on the table and swept out a hand. "Everything will be just fine," he said, carefully extracting the creature from the folds of his palm and flicking it into the chimney of the lamp on the table. "You just wait."

"You never said anything about blowing up the dam. Don't you know there is more than just a little stock pond backed up behind it? When Jim Kincade built that dam, he flooded miles of canyons. The water from that thing could wipe out a town!"

"There ain't no town below the dam, Martin," Jenney pointed out.

"The Kincades have their cattle grazing in the valley,

and men too. Martha has told me more than once their best pastureland is along the Old River."

Burt grinned as the fly in the lamp flared like a torch. "That's right. Over five hundred head are fattening on that tall riverbottom grass right this minute."

Caldwell's eyes widened. "You mean to drown them!"

"I said *I'd* take care of the Kincades. Your job is not to worry about how, but to take care of all the legalities and paperwork. I'll see to my end. You see to yours."

Caldwell wheeled away and looked out the window at the darkening street below. The glow of a lamp being lighted in the undertaker's parlor down the street caught his eye. Shadows moved behind the dingy windows. Two men came out the door to lift something from the back of a carriage and carry it inside. He paid it little attention. At the moment more pressing thoughts occupied his mind. He drew a breath of cool night air and slowly returned his attention to the stuffy second-floor room above the bank where Burt Jenney was casually filling the air with thick, gray clouds of cigar smoke.

"Okay, Burt, okay," he said after thinking it over. "I only wish there was some other way."

"I do, too, Martin, you know that. Blowing the dam and killing all those animals gives me no great pleasure, but it's the only way we're going to break that old lady once and for all. If we allow her to continue selling off bits and pieces of that ranch to those farmers, it could be years before she defaults on the notes we hold. By that time there won't be anything left of the Largo. A hundred different farmers will own it all!" Burt Jenney leaned back in the chair.

The even beat of the hall clock seemed to punctuate

the long moments that passed. The stuffy, smoke-laden air in the little apartment only added to the banker's sudden depression.

"If there was only some other way, Burt. But of course you are correct. The longer Martha Kincade is allowed to parcel out bits and pieces of her ranch, the less valuable it becomes. All right," Caldwell said, drawing up a chair. "What's your plan?"

Burt took the cigar from his teeth and grinned, as if this small victory was particularly satisfying. "A couple of the Double T boys that work for me are riding out to the Kincade place tonight."

"Can they be trusted?"

Jenney gave a short laugh. "I've enough on them to guarantee a rope around their neck if they cross us up. We can trust them."

"And they on you, I should think. What about Old Man Tyrell?"

"He doesn't know a thing about it."

Caldwell caught a loose fingernail between his teeth.

"After they blow the dam, and what's left of the Largo herd is scattered, Martha Kincade will be flat broke. She'll come to the bank—you, Caldwell—for another loan." Jenney smiled. "But of course you won't be able to give her any more money because of all the notes already outstanding. Being the prudent business-man you are, you'll tell her you cannot justify lending her any more of the bank's money. However"—Jenney paused as Martin Caldwell raked his lower lip with his teeth—"if she will agree to sign over the deeds to the bank, you can give her ten thousand, a fair price for the land considering what she already owes and the fact that there won't be much in the way of cattle left to sell. If she accepts the money, you will call it even with the bank." Burt raised an eyebrow and waited for Caldwell's reply.

"It won't work. Martha Kincade would rather die than sell out!"

"Of course she'll sell, Martin. She's bullheaded, but she ain't stupid! If it was only herself she had to worry about, it would be different. But it's not *only* herself. She'd sell heaven and hell for that daughter of hers. Valerie costs money. Money Martha isn't making by holding onto a losing proposition like the Largo. She'll hem and haw, and call you a thief, but in the end she'll sign the papers and take the money—our money, and we'll have the Largo."

Martin got up slowly from the table, walked across the room, and gazed at the ceiling. The steady ticking of the clock sounded unusually loud in the quiet room. "Okay," he said finally, still looking at the ceiling, "do whatever you think necessary."

Caldwell turned away abruptly and hung his head out the open window as if the clean air outside could expurgate the corruption inside himself. The nightly hullabaloo from the Silver Lady Saloon rose up from the dark street below. The hitching rails in front of the saloon were filled, and riders were tying up farther down the street now, wandering in pairs or singly through the batwing doors, casting their long shadows into the street.

He glanced again at the carriage in front of the undertaker's parlor. "Jenney, come here."

"Huh?" The sheriff came out of the chair and hung his head out the window. "What is it?"

Four had men started up the street. Caldwell recognized the big man among them, Dave Thompson. The men disappeared into the shadows of an alley, reappeared on the sidewalk, and stopped at the jailhouse door. Thompson pounded the door and waited. Caldwell said, "I saw them come from Strathmore's place. They carried a body in earlier."

Jenney frowned. "Those are Largo men, and that's Bracken with them. I'd better see what they want." Burt snatched his hat from the table. At the door he stopped and said, "I'll talk with you later, Martin," and hurried down the outside stairs.

Jenney crushed his cigar in the ashtray on his desk and leaned back in his chair, regarding the four men standing before him. His gaze riveted on Langely, and he said, "You're sure it was Hank Acker you saw, Bracken?"

"That's what I said, Sheriff." Jenney's reluctance to believe him was beginning to annoy Langely.

"Murder is a serious accusation."

Langely let that go without comment.

Jenney nodded his head slowly. "Now, you say these six men were waiting for you down by the Porter River crossing?"

Dave Thompson leaned forward and anchored his fist on Jenney's desktop. "Damn it all, Burt, why this nitpicking. The fact is Joe Lascoe is dead. Murdered! And it could have easily been Valerie or Thomas. What the hell are you waiting for? Arrest Hank Acker and find out who those other men with him were!"

Burt rocked back in his chair. "Hold on, Dave. I can't go running out and arrest a man on the word of a stranger. At least not before I know all the facts. Considering the trouble Bracken and Hank had last night, how do I know this fellow ain't trying to get at Acker through this incident?"

Langely was suddenly aware of Thompson's arm reaching out to stop him, and that his fists were clenched. It half surprised him that he had made a move at the sheriff, and that Jenney had started out of the chair too. Jenney halted his retreat and settled back down, but he kept a wary eye on Langely.

"We have Valerie's word too!" Dave said.

"But Valerie isn't here," Jenney pointed out, a cautious eye turned at Langely.

"She was too upset to come back into town."

Jenney nodded his head. "I can understand that, Dave, but I'm going to need her testimony to—"

"In the meantime, Sheriff," Langely said in a restrained voice, "you're going to let Acker walk the streets?"

Burt sighed, and looked at him, then over to Dave. He grimaced, and said in a tired voice, "Dave, I've known you a good many years. You're a trustworthy man. Not many around I can truthfully say that about. For that reason alone I'll listen to this stranger. I'll go out and see if I can find Acker—on your word, Dave— but if what Bracken says is true, I doubt very much the man will be hanging around town." Jenney went to the rack of rifles on the wall, took down a Winchester, and began to pump bullets into the magazine. "I want to see Valerie in the morning, to verify all this, hear?"

"I'll bring her around," Dave agreed.

Outside, Jenney put out a hand and stopped Langely. "Bracken, don't leave town anytime soon."

"Why, Sheriff? I didn't kill anyone. You just see to it

you get the men who did." The two men eyed each other.

Jenney said through a frozen smile, "I don't like what I hear in your voice. If you're thinking of taking the law into your own hands, I'd advise against it." He patted the palm of his hand with the barrel of the Winchester, then turned away and walked up the street. At the Silver Lady Saloon he stopped and glanced back before pushing through the swinging doors.

"Ain't never seen Burt like that before," Dave said, shaking his head.

"Burt and old Joe, they go back a long ways together," Bill Tremely said.

"Maybe that's it." Dave paused as if giving the notion some thought. "Me and the boys are heading back to the ranch tonight, Thomas, why don't you ride along with us?"

Langely grinned, "You heard the sheriff, I'm not to leave town. I wouldn't want to ruffle Burt Jenney's feathers any more than I already have. Thanks anyway."

Dave found a smile somewhere deep within himself. "No, we wouldn't want to do that. I'll bring Valerie by in the morning. She'll most likely want you along when she talks to Burt."

"I'll be here."

They walked back to Strathmore's together to collect their horses and the carriage. Dave and his men mounted up and started out of town. Langely climbed into his saddle and turned his horse toward the livery stable at the other end of town. As he passed the saloon, he reined in and peered over the batwing doors into the smoky barroom. Burt Jenney was standing by the bar talking with someone there—one of the men that had picked a fight with him that morning. As he watched, Jenney pushed away from the bar and left the saloon by a side door.

Thinking it over, Langely had the feeling that scattered pieces of a large puzzle were somehow coming together, although he had no idea what the final picture would look like. But something was brewing, and if he didn't miss his guess, that something was about to bust wide open. He continued to the livery and unsaddled, hayed, and curried his horse.

A half hour later as he walked back toward the Montgomery Hotel, he saw that a light was still burning in Lemont's office. The door was unlocked, and on a notion he stepped inside.

14

Albert Canon heaved himself away from the bar with a bottle in hand and a vacant stare in his red eyes. Like a homeless dog, he wandered from table to table until he found an empty chair. "Deal me in," he said, and proceeded to fill the four glasses there.

Calvin Dexter looked up from the cards he was shuffling and said, "What did the sheriff want, Al?"

Canon shrugged, "He was just killing some time. Deal me a good one, Cal."

"With a Winchester tucked under his arm?" Calvin grinned. "First I ever heard of a man killing time with a rifle!" The men chuckled as they collected their cards.

Lisa Wingate swung by the table and leaned over Calvin's shoulder. "Which one of you boys is winning tonight?" she cooed, batting painted eyes at the men.

"Jeff's taking our money tonight, Lisa," Brad said.

Jeff Tyrell's face colored when Lisa gave him a generous smile. She circled the table and slid a hand over his shoulder. "How about a drink, Mr. Tyrell?"

Jeff pretended not to hear their muffled laughter. It was a game all the girls at the Silver Lady Saloon played. No one minded them begging drinks—or what followed later in the evening if a man had his mind set in that direction.

"Sure sweetheart. Bartender! A drink for the lady!"

A girl brought the drink by, collected Jeff's money, and gave Lisa a wink. Lisa draped herself around the table until she was certain the men were more interested in playing cards than playing the game she could offer and gracefully slipped away to try another table.

The cards moved around the table, and Lisa was forgotten—except by Canon. She had rekindled the fire that seeing Sarah Lawrence's shapely leg had sparked inside him earlier—a sudden warming that had nothing to do with all the whiskey he'd put down that day. All at once the card game was an annoying distraction. An unimportant blur that kept him from concentrating fully on more lusty desires. At the end of the hand Al kicked back his chair and got up.

"Where are you going?" Jeff Tyrell asked.

"The air in here's getting too stuffy, and anyway I'm all out of money. I'm going out for a while."

"Don't go getting into any more trouble. Tomorrow it's back to the ranch and work," Jeff told him.

"Don't worry, Mr. Tyrell, I ain't gonna get into trouble, just going out for some air." Outside he stopped on the sidewalk and took a deep breath to clear his head. He braced himself as the sidewalk pitched beneath him and rolled like the deck of a ship at sea. Steadying his legs, he lurched headlong toward the general store and stopped at its windows to glance into the darkened building. From the open doorway at the rear came a pale-yellow light and the flicker of shadows on the back wall. Canon's heart pounded. Beads pricked his forehead. The cool night air brought a shudder to his sweaty body as he gulped down the last of the whiskey and flung the bottle down the dark alley.

His fingers tingled as they touched the door handle and it swung open effortlessly. Casting a glance along the empty street, Canon's thin lips curled back, and he slipped quickly inside, quietly closing the door behind him.

A gently hummed melody drifted from the back room.

Canon found the shade cords in the dark and pulled them down.

Sarah Lawrence had been unwrapping a brown-paper bundle and humming softly to herself, when the uneasy feeling came over her. She stopped, turned around, and a startled cry caught in her throat.

"How did you get in here?"

Canon braced himself in the doorway, slowly feeling Sarah's slender body with his brooding eyes.

She grasped her shoulder with her other hand and moved her arm modestly across herself. "How did you get in here!" she demanded.

Canon nodded toward the door. "It was open. I figured you were expectin' someone—me?" He grinned and pushed himself straight in the doorway.

Sarah stared past him at the front door, closed now and bolted. The shades were drawn over the windows too.

Canon glanced at the cot in the corner of the room, then back at her. "Don't fret none, little lady. We have the whole night. You might even enjoy it. I guarantee no one will bother us." He loosened the dirty neckerchief from his throat and stepped into the room.

Marcus Lemont lowered himself into a chair, shaking his head. He looked suddenly older and very tired. "Joe . . . dead? I can't believe it." When he looked up, his eyes were moist. "That old man wouldn't hurt a fly. I just don't understand why . . ." Lemont's voice hardened. "Hank Acker, you say? You saw him?"

Langely said, "He was one of the six who jumped us. I didn't recognize any of the others."

"Why didn't Jenney lock that man in jail last night when he had the chance?"

"He didn't. There is no profit in wondering what-if. Joe is dead." Langely's sudden bitterness was directed at himself as well. He'd had his chance at Hank Acker and let it pass.

Lemont's face twisted. "By thunder, what's Jenney doing about it?"

"The sheriff is reluctant to do anything. He agreed to look for Acker, but made it plain enough he didn't expect to find him." A frown found its way to Langely's face. "I find that kind of strange behavior for a man who, according to Bill Tremely, was a friend of Joe's—a longtime friend."

Lemont nodded. "Longtime friends—that they were. Both men worked for Big Jim Kincade before the trouble began. Even after Jenney left the ranch and took to sheriffing, those two kept in with each other."

Langely's eyebrows came together. "Burt Jenney used to work for the Largo?"

"About fifteen years ago."

"Did Jenney quit before or after Jim Kincade was killed?"

"Quit?" Something vaguely like amusement came to Lemont's face, and then just as swiftly it passed. "Let's see, if my memory serves me he *quit* some time before Jim Kincade was killed. Why do you ask?"

Thomas Langely didn't know why he had asked, but something he recalled hearing earlier that morning nagged at him. He was putting pieces of a puzzle together with no clear notion what picture would form. "I've learned so much Esteros Creek history in the two days I've been in town that I'm just naturally getting curious."

Marcus Lemont indicated the back room of his office. "I have fourteen years of Esteros Creek history piled nearly to the ceiling back there, Thomas. If you ever get a bad case of the curiosity itch, that's the place to start scratching it. You're welcome to dig through that mountain of newsprint anytime—I do it often. You'd be surprised the kernels of useful information one finds scattered among the humdrum of Esteros Creek's dreary past."

Lemont rose from his chair and shuffled back behind a long table, where he had been setting up the type for the next edition. He stared down at it and shook his head. "This will all have to be changed," he said somberly. "I rant and rave about the somnolent, fundamentally newsless hunk of real estate we call Esteros Creek, and joke about a newspaper surviving in a town that generates no news above the gossip-column level, but

ALL YOURS FREE!

Old West with
mpelling novel, *Sackett*,
e!

You may keep *Sackett* for only $4.95!*

*plus shipping and handling, and sales tax in NY and Canada.

In Addition to the Free Louis L'Amour Calenda

. . . your risk-free preview volume of *Sackett* will introduce you to these
outstanding qualities of the bookbinder's art—

- Each volume is bound in rich, rugged sierra-brown simulated leather.

- The bindings are sewn, not just glued, to last a lifetime. And the pages are
  printed on high-quality paper that is acid-free and will not yellow with age

- The title and Louis L'Amour's signature are golden embossed on the spine
  and front cover of each volume.

it's times like this that that old adage is unimpeachable
—No news is good news." Lemont began breaking
down the type block.

"Last night you said you wanted to talk."

"I did?" Lemont went on with his work without looking up. "Oh, yes, of course. Where was it you said you
came from, I can't seem to recall?"

"I didn't, not exactly."

"The East, I believe."

"That covers a lot of territory."

"You're being cryptic."

"A man's past is his own affair."

Lemont peered up from the table and nodded his
head. "A man has a right to hide his past—if he truly
wants to. Tell me, Mr. Bracken, do you know anything
about guns?"

Langely studied the newspaperman, uneasy about
where this line of questioning might be taking him. "A
little. Enough to fill the pot every now and then. I like to
hunt birds whenever I get the chance."

"Then you have considerably more knowledge on the
subject than I." Lemont put down the block of type and
went to his desk. He produced a pistol from the top
drawer. "A . . . er . . . gentleman gave this to me a
while back. Tell me what you think of it."

Langely took the gun and eyed Lemont suspiciously.
It was an 1873 model Colt Army revolver marked .44
WCF on the barrel. He thumbed the hammer to half
cock, listened as the pawl indexed with the ratchets, and
checked the cylinders. They were empty. He cocked the
piece all the way, snapped the hammer, then handed it
back to Lemont.

"It appears to be new, but why ask me? There's a gun shop in town. I'm sure you can get an appraisal there."

The newspaperman said, "Indeed I could, but they would tell me what I already know. The gun is new. Fired maybe a dozen times at a row of whiskey bottles out back. I have a vast supply of empty whiskey bottles. They'd tell me it was still in excellent condition, just as when they sold it to me last year." Lemont grinned. "You see, I lied about it being a gift. It was only a test, Mr. Langely."

So easily did the name flow off Lemont's tongue that Thomas almost didn't catch it. The silence stretched for a dozen heartbeats. "That didn't take you long," he said.

Lemont laid a finger aside his nose and tapped it twice. "It's trained to sniff out news," he said, "and when a famous *pistolero* rides into our sleepy village without his gun—well, that's news."

Lemont left the typesetting table and unfolded a yellowed newspaper on his desk dated two years previous. The front page displayed a poorly defined line drawing of Thomas Langely, and beneath it a short article chronicling the latest adventures of the famous gunman.

Langely glanced at the paper. "Now you have two interesting bits of front-page news for your paper."

"I still only have one, Thomas. You're absolutely right. A man's past should be his own affair. Your secret won't get out through my newspaper."

Marcus Lemont went back to the typesetting table and resumed his work. Langely sat slowly back in the newspaperman's chair. He had expected his past to catch up with him eventually, but he hadn't expected it this soon. He had hoped enough years would have gone by to make it unimportant.

Lemont interrupted his thoughts. "You are probably already aware of this, Thomas, but if you had accepted Acker's challenge yesterday, all that happened today might have been avoided."

Langely shot out of the chair. "Why do you think I left Montana?" He was suddenly angry, as if that could change anything. "It was because living had gotten to the point where I couldn't walk out my door without some wet-behind-the-ears, self-styled gunhand trying to use me as a springboard to a ready-made reputation! Yes, I could have killed Acker last night. And I had a real good hunch those riders would be waiting for us too. But I didn't do a damn thing about it! Those men weren't shooting at Joe. They were shooting at *us*! It could just as easily be Valerie lying on that slab down at Strathmore's."

"Or you."

Langely spun away to face the wall, his broad back swelling beneath the dark vest. "And what am I doing about it now? Nothing! Not one damn thing! You want to know why?" He turned back. "I'll tell you. I'm scared! Scared that if I strap on a gun, it's going to start all over again—the killings, the constant watch over my shoulder, not being able to eat in peace without placing my back against a wall. . . ."

He let his anger die as suddenly as it had come on and dropped back into the chair, rapping his fingers on Lemont's desk.

"I should not have brought it up," Lemont said.

"Why?" Langely pulled his hat down on his head. "It's the truth." He started for the door.

"What you say is true, Thomas. You have the right to a life of peace, but so do other folks that can't protect themselves against men like Hank Acker. You know, being good with a gun isn't evil. It's the way you put that ability to use determines the good or bad of it.

"The Kincades are decent folks, but they are only an old lady and a young girl, and someone or something is turning this town against them. I don't know what it is, but I can feel it, and I suspect you can too."

"And you expect me to straighten out the trouble?"

"What I'm trying to say is this; your reticence to use your gun again is honorable, but at this point in time it may not be the best course of action, not when people—good people—need your help. The decision of course is yours to make, but think about this: Sometimes a silent gun can cause more harm than good."

He had much to think about when he left Lemont's office. Ever since his arrival in Esteros Creek he had second-guessed himself, had allowed others to determine his actions—a thing he'd never tolerated before.

Lemont was correct when he said something was brewing. He felt it even after only two days in town. He recalled Sarah's coolness toward him and Burt Jenney's reluctance to take action against Hank Acker. Of all the people he'd met so far, only Marcus Lemont and Dave Thompson appeared genuinely open and honest. Everyone else was either acting or reacting under some strain.

Joe's death was only a start of bigger trouble, he was sure. He grimaced. It had been an unfortunate time to ride into Esteros Creek, but here he was, and something inside him wanted to stay. It was time he started picking sides.

He thought of Sarah Lawrence then. Why was she so put off by him while he felt so compelled—?

Without warning his thoughts were torn away by the muffled cry of a woman. He stopped, and his eyes swept over the darkened storefronts, but the night remained quiet, the cry lost in its silence.

15

Langely was certain he had heard a woman cry out, and
as he lunged across the street, he was convinced the cry
had come from the general store. The door was locked.
He pressed his face against the dark glass and saw only
that the shades had been drawn, but the sounds of scuf-
fling inside reached his ears like the rustle of dry paper.

He brought his heel up, and the door groaned beneath it, splintering as the lock ripped from the jam. In
the next room shadows wrestled across the wall. Langely
plunged into it and took in the scene in a single glance.
Sarah's blouse was ripped from shoulder to waist, and
Canon's fingers were tearing at the one last flimsy white
petticoat left. Langely's grip came down onto Canon's
shoulder like the tightening of a vise and wrenched him
away from her.

A moment of surprise spread across Canon's face an
instant before Langely's fist crashed into it. He stum-

bled back against the wall. Langely moved in, shattered Canon's jaw with one blow, ground his nose to a pulp with a second. He restrained the urge to hit him again and let Canon slip from his fingers to the floor. When he turned back, Sarah's wide eyes stared out from the corner of the room where she huddled.

"You all right, Sarah?" he asked.

She nodded, clutching the ribboned remains of the blouse to herself.

The man at his feet groaned. Langely heaved him to his feet and held him against the wall. "I know you, mister, you were in on that little fight this morning outside the saloon."

Canon's eyes rolled as he tried to speak, but blood filled his mouth, and his tongue stumbled over the new openings where a few moments earlier teeth had resided.

"You're a friend of Hank Acker's, aren't you? Aren't you!" Langely demanded when it appeared Canon was slipping toward unconsciousness.

"Yeah . . . yeah, I . . . Hank's friend . . ." Canon's jaw didn't work too well.

"Were you with him this morning when he and five others killed Joe Lascoe?"

Behind him he heard Sarah gasp. He had not wanted her to find out this way.

Canon shook his head and sputtered something that sounded like no.

"Where is Acker now?"

Canon's eyes widened. "I . . . I don't know," he mumbled, his speaking hampered by the broken jaw.

Langely reached into the top of his boot, and a short blade flickered in the lamplight. He pressed the blade close to Canon's face. "I've no more patience left. You'll answer my questions, and I don't give a damn how much it hurts to talk. Where is Hank Acker?"

Canon hesitated a moment too long. The little knife opened a gash under his chin, and he cried out like a wounded dog.

"I've skinned lots of rattlesnakes in my day, but never a man. You want to be my first?"

Canon sputtered as fast as his broken jaw would move. "Hank . . . out to the Largo . . ." His words trailed off in a sheet of pain.

"The Largo?" Langely glanced at Sarah, but her overstretched eyes and drawn-back lips told him only of her terror.

"What's he doing out at the Largo?"

"The dam . . . ," he gurgled, choking on the blood that filled his mouth.

"The dam? What dam?"

"In . . . Porter Canyon," he managed to say.

Langely recalled Valerie briefly mentioning a dam her father had built. "What's Acker going to do at the dam?"

"Blow . . . blow it up." Canon raised an unsteady hand to wipe away the blood streaming down his chin. He seemed to drift away from consciousness, and for an instant his eyes rolled up.

Langely shook him awake. "Why is he going to blow up the dam?"

"Don't know . . ." Canon said, his eyes blinking at the short blade in Langely's hand. Panic played upon his tortured face. "Don't know . . . don't know," he said frantically. "Orders . . ."

"Whose orders?" There was an edge of urgency in

Langely's voice, for he could see that Canon was falling back into unconsciousness.

Canon's head tipped to his chest.

"Who ordered him?" Langely was yelling now.

Canon's eyes rolled up in his head, and his lids closed. Langely lowered him to the floor and turned to Sarah.

She started to come to him, but hesitated. He took her into his arms, and she came suddenly willingly into them. "It's all over," he said, pulling her gently to himself. "It's all over."

She trembled a long time, then disengaged herself from his hold and hugged herself modestly. She looked at her ruined clothing. He found a shawl folded across a chair, wrapped it around Sarah's shoulders, and sat her down in the chair. She produced a handkerchief and dried her eyes.

"Is it true? Is Joe really dead?"

He nodded his head.

"Hank Acker killed him?"

"I don't know whose bullet did the killing, Sarah. Six men laid for us along the road to the Largo. One of them was Acker. I didn't recognize the others."

"How is Val? She and Joe were so very close."

"Both Valerie and her mother handled it like women who have seen death before."

Sarah looked up. "They would. Strong people, the Kincades are." Sarah's voice turned urgent. "What did he mean about blowing up the dam?"

"I don't know," he said, and he was aware of a twinge of regret. All his hopes for a new life were being quickly eroded by the river of events that had caught him up and was now carrying him away. He considered the lovely woman before him and knew a more bitter regret.

"I'll wait while you change your clothes," he said. "Then I'll ride out to the Largo. You can report this to the sheriff. I think I ought to be out of town when he finds out about this."

Sarah was about to speak, when she glanced past his shoulder, and her eyes suddenly went wide. "Thomas, behind you!"

Langely leaped aside, taking Sarah with him. The roar of the revolver in the small room was deafening. The chair Sarah had been sitting in an instant before rocked back and splintered apart. Langely pushed Sarah out of the line of fire as Canon thumbed back the hammer for a second shot. He flipped over the little knife he still held, catching the blade between his fingers. The sliver of steel flickered across the room. A cry of disbelief escaped Canon's mouth as he stared at the hilt of the knife stuck to the front of his shirt. The revolver slipped from his fingers, and a moment later Canon followed it to the floor.

Langely rolled Canon to his back and extracted the thin boot knife.

"Is he dead?" Sarah whispered through her cupped fingers. The shawl had fallen half off her bare shoulders.

"He's dead," Langely said grimly. Although it was self-defense, he knew he stood little chance of trying to talk his way out of Burt Jenney's jail now. A face poked through the hanging front door, then a second as gawkers, attracted off the street by the gunshot, began to arrive. Lemont was among them, and his breath smelled of whiskey as he ventured into the room, but his words were stone sober.

"My God," he said, stopping just inside. "What happened here?" His view swept over the blood-splattered walls.

Langely helped Sarah out of the room and said to Lemont, "Take care of her, Marc. Get her a room at the hotel. She can't stay here tonight."

"And you?" Lemont asked.

"I have to ride out to the Largo." He scooped his hat from the floor and pushed through the crowd at the front door, out into the night air.

16

Moonlight through the open window reflected dully off the revolver in Thomas Langely's hand. His saddlebags lay open upon the bed, empty now, and as he studied the gun, he grimaced. It had been futile to try to change what he was. For too many years he'd cut a broad swath through life, dealing with the world on his terms—a strong fist and a fast gun. It was too late to change all that now.

He buckled the gun belt around his waist. Other towns waited down the road, and maybe someday he might try it again—but he doubted it.

Langely left the room with his Winchester and saddlebags in hand. Sarah and Lemont were in the lobby when he came down the stairs.

She came to him, clutching the shawl around her, and looked at the gun on his hip, confused. He read the question that had come suddenly to her eyes. He was, after all, the man who had claimed to have had no use for handguns.

"I don't have time to explain now, Sarah," he said gently and looked to Lemont. "Marcus . . . ?"

The newspaperman nodded his head. Lemont would tell her the hard truth he had hoped would not come out so soon. Langely's view was drawn back to Sarah's face. Her blue eyes were suddenly soft and understanding, not bitter and reproachful as he had expected. She put out a hand and touched his. "Be careful, Thomas."

His arms ached to pull her to him and hold her forever, but that could never be now. He started past her toward the door, when Jenney stepped inside, blocking his way. In a glance each man measured the other.

"I warned you about taking the law into your own hands. I'm going to have to take you in."

"I can't let you do that, Sheriff," Langely said in an even voice, but the menacing tone was something he had never learned to hide.

Jenney noticed the gun on his hip then. His stare narrowed, and his hand eased toward the revolver on his hip. Langely watched from cool gray eyes.

Lemont cleared his throat. "Ah, Sheriff, you don't really want to do that—"

"Stay out of this, Lemont!" Jenney snapped, still watching Langely.

Marcus Lemont took Sarah's arm and stepped away from the two men. Edwin squeezed out from behind the desk and hurried to the next room, poking an eye around the doorway.

"Mr. Bracken," Jenney said, "I expect you to hand that gun over to me . . . or use it. The choice is yours."

"I can't hand it over, Sheriff," he said, "so . . ." His

words trailed off, and suddenly the Colt was in his hand, pointing at Jenney's chest.

He heard Sarah gasp. Jenney's face turned to stone at the sudden appearance of the revolver.

". . . I guess I'm going to have to use it," Langely finished easily.

"Mister, you're makin' a lot more trouble for yourself."

"I've been there before, Sheriff. Sarah, come get his gun."

She balked. Burt Jenney was the law, after all.

"Sarah," he said sharply, "I have no time to waste."

She looked at Burt, then at the revolver in Langely's hand, and turned a pleading eye to Lemont. The newspaperman nodded his head. Sarah drew the heavy revolver from Jenney's holster and put it in Langely's hand.

Langely eyed it, seeing it clearly for the first time, and grinned. Something murky had suddenly come into focus. "An interesting sidearm, Sheriff," he said. "An eighteen fifty-one Navy Colt with a Richard-Mason conversion. I haven't seen one like this in years. In fact not since right after the war." He glanced at Lemont. "They used to convert these old cap-and-ball pistols to fire the then-new metallic cartridges," he said, handing the gun over to him. "Here is one for *you* to examine. When you finish, I suggest digging through that back room of yours for another interesting *kernel* of information—try about the time Jim Kincade was killed."

Lemont took the gun, confused, and turned it over in his hands.

"Will you watch the sheriff for me while I get my horse?"

"I can't do that, Thomas." Lemont looked uncertainly from Langely to Jenney. "Burt's our sheriff. By all that is right I should be trying to stop you. Don't ask me to help in this!"

It was Lemont's town, and he had to live in it. Langely understood. He said to Jenney, "Let's take a walk across the street." Jenney hesitated and then turned outside, and they angled across the street into the jailhouse.

"Where do you keep the keys?"

"On the wall, behind the desk."

Langely retrieved the heavy ring. "I know you have a second set, where are they?"

Jenney nodded to his desk. "Top left. I don't suppose I can talk you out of this foolishness, Bracken?"

"I don't suppose you can," Langely said, waving his revolver at the cell block. The old iron door sang on dry hinges, and the lock clunked heavily into place.

"I'll throw these keys in the watering trough at the livery. You can have someone fetch them once I'm clear of town. Don't send anyone after me that you want to stay alive."

At the livery he flung the keys into a trough and saddled up his horse. He led the animal from the dark building and stopped in the street when Sarah walk out from the shadows.

"Thomas." She hesitated. "I . . . I wanted to see you before you left." The words came with effort, and she clutched the shawl tighter, as if to draw strength from it. Eyes half hidden in the shadows of her face searched his for some kind of reassurance.

He dropped the reins, and suddenly Sarah was in his arms. He pulled her close and kissed her hard. Her soft lips surrendered to his, her body yielded beneath his strong arms.

"Oh, Thomas," she said, putting her head to his chest, "I've been so afraid of my feelings since I first saw you."

They held each other in the pale shroud of a large moon, and after a little while he gently removed Sarah's arms from around his waist. "I have to go, but I'll be back."

"Lemont told me," she said, gathering the ends of the shawl that had fallen open. "It doesn't matter, your past I mean, I understand."

He swung into his saddle, looked down at Sarah Lawrence, and knew he had fallen hopelessly under her spell.

"Please help the Kincades."

He grimaced. The lines were drawn, and the sides chosen. "I'm going to try," he said, and kicked the horse into motion.

17

Will Tanner swung off his horse and hunkered down by the fire to pour himself a cup of coffee from a blackened pot. It was a small fire, too small to attract the attention of the wranglers camped in the river valley across the ridge, and when the sun dropped below the horizon, the flames would be broken up and only the coals allowed to glow. Tanner arched his back and said, "Damn, we've been doing a lot of riding today."

Manning looked up from where he was lazing against four crates of dynamite and nodded his dark head toward Acker and Lowe. "They wanted to see you as soon as you got back, *pronto*," he said.

"I'll bet they do." Tanner tied his horse to a small juniper along with the others and kicked through the stiff grass. He hunched down beside Acker and Lowe. "Well . . . ? What did you see?"

Tanner viewed Acker over the rim of his cup. "There

ain't much going on, Hank. Looks to me like most the men are off somewhere. But that valley is full of cattle, for sure."

"How many men did you see?"

"I counted only three."

"Three?" Lowe said, and frowned. "I don't like it. Only three men to watch over a herd that large? It don't sound right to me."

"Five years ago Old Lady Kincade would have had maybe eight or ten men watching her animals," Acker said, "but now it's different. She's on to hard times."

Lowe tasted the last of his coffee, made a face, and splashed the cold liquid onto a rock. "And times are about to get a whole lot harder." He tapped the grinds from the bottom of his cup. "Three men. That makes what we got to do easy, like shooting ducks on a pond."

"Yeah, easy," Tanner said, but his voice was troubled. "I just hope those men aren't standing along that old riverbed when the dam goes."

Lowe shrugged. "Three less Largo hands to worry about."

"Jenney didn't want nobody hurt," Acker said, and he sounded troubled too.

"If Burt don't want nobody hurt, let him come out here and do his own dirty work, otherwise we do the job our way!" Lowe stood and went to the fire.

Tanner glanced at Acker when Lowe had left. "I don't trust him sometimes. He likes killing too much."

Acker looked over at the fire where Lowe was filling his coffee cup. "He's okay," he said, but there wasn't much conviction in it.

* * *

Four hours after the sun had died against a black horizon, Hank Acker kicked dirt over the coals and said, "It's time. Get that dynamite loaded up."

They loaded the crates onto two horses and started down the back side of the ridge. Acker had scouted the trail earlier, and in the pallid night light they followed it into a deep ravine, where junipers and piñons snagged their legs and arms. Up on the other side they dismounted and peered over the canyon rim.

A rock-and-earthen dam stretched darkly across the deep narrows below. Behind the dam a black-glass surface snaked up the canyon and in scattered places threw back moonlight. The men unloaded the dynamite and hauled the explosives down the long talus incline to the top of the dam.

"That should hold it until morning, Miss Lawrence."

"Thank you," she said as the workman gathered up his tools and returned them to his hand box.

"I'll be by in the morning to repair those hinges and the lock in a proper fashion," he said. "In the meantime you'll have no trouble with vandals tonight. But you will have to use the back door." He tested his repair job and seemed satisfied. "Yep, that should do till the morrow. Good night, Miss Lawrence."

When he had left, Lemont escorted her down the dark alleyway to the back of the store. Inside, she paused among the shattered furniture and blood-smeared walls. A shudder gripped her, and she closed her eyes until it passed.

"I won't be but a minute, Marcus," she said, submerging the memory of that evening beneath the ocean of new emotions that had surfaced since Thomas Langely had come to town—emotions that had suddenly, and frighteningly, made themselves clear to her for the first time only an hour ago. She hurried through another door and up a flight of stairs to her rooms on the second floor. In five minutes she had packed all that she would need for the night and left, grateful to be away from the scene of violence and death—at least until the morning, when she would have to confront the disarray and put it right, including mopping the blood, which for the moment was a task beyond her fortitude.

Lemont walked her back to the hotel and bid her good night. Afterward she sat in the comforting circle of light from the lamp on the dresser.

Enough of this!

She had spent ample time feeling sorry for herself, and that was not her nature. She set about getting ready for bed. Tomorrow would be a heavy day, and she needed her sleep.

Sarah extinguished the lamp and crawled between the sheets, but sleep evaded her. And it wasn't the store or seeing Albert Canon killed that kept her awake. It was the thought of a certain man, a stranger, really, until only a few hours ago.

The why of it eluded her. What was different about this man, and why would she find it appealing? There certainly was no lack of suitors in a town like Esteros Creek, where men outnumbered women by an easy five score. So why should she find Thomas Langely attractive? Was it his quiet strength? His patience with her, even after she had publicly spurned him? Or perhaps it was what he was trying to do with his life? She gave a short laugh in the dark and told herself it was only infatuation. He had come to her rescue—a knight in shining armor—seen through eyes too tired to discern the reality from fantasy, and in the morning all this would be an embarrassing memory, to be secreted away in a closet named Foolish Youth.

As she lay there thinking these things, a commotion out on the street drew her from her bed to the window.

"Unhand me! I demand an explanation!" Lemont was saying in the street below.

The sheriff ignored Lemont's plea as he hauled him along by the sleeve of his black coat into the jailhouse across the street.

Puzzled, Sarah watched the busy shadows behind the shades, hearing Lemont's indignant outbursts until the shadows moved away from the window. In a few minutes the lights across the street went out, and Jenney reappeared on the sidewalk, locking the door behind him. He stood there a moment, studying the long, empty street. Except for the saloon's constant din, like a noise the brain learns to mask out, the town was quiet as a graveyard. He walked back across the street. Sarah was thankful she had extinguished the lamp and she felt secure in the darkness of her hotel window as she watched the sheriff linger on the sidewalk in front of the bank. As if reassuring himself that no one was watching, Jenney ducked into the alleyway and skipped up the side stairs. Sarah heard his urgent rapping, and it was then that she first noticed that a lamp was still lit in the rooms above the bank. Caldwell's rooms.

The door opened at his knock, and as if one step ahead of Mephistopheles himself, Jenney ducked inside and the door closed immediately.

Sarah waited, but Jenney never reemerged. With an apprehension for Lemont to further lengthen her list of concerns, she returned to bed, her thoughts, and a sleepless night. . . .

Valerie moved her food around the plate with her fork. A glance told her that her mother had no stomach for food either. After a few minutes the old woman pushed her plate aside and sat with a vacant look in her eyes.

"Are you all right, Mother?" Valerie asked, setting her fork down. The death of Joe Lascoe had weighed heavy on both of them all day.

Martha nodded slowly. "I'm feeling a bit tired, dear, but I'm all right."

The house seemed unbearably stuffy. Valerie excused herself and went outside, but the oppressive gloom followed her out the front door. When she stepped back inside, her mother had already begun to clean up the dishes. Valerie made a move to help, but she stopped herself. They both needed to be alone with their thoughts, and she knew it no longer bothered Martha to tend the household chores. She had had her day of easy living in the big house Jim had built for her. In those days Martha Kincade was a woman of means, with four domestics to cook and clean and see to the needs of her and her family—but that was all gone now. Martha had often said how fitting it was to be ending out her life as she had started it, a hardworking woman.

Valerie knew that what bothered her mother wasn't that she could no longer afford the luxuries of life. What nettled Martha Kincade was her lack of control over the Largo. The Largo had been the biggest thing in the territory when Jim had been alive, but she was not the businessman Big Jim had been. No matter how hard she tried, the Largo crept steadily toward decay—that's what bothered Martha Kincade.

Valerie took a book to a chair in the corner, but after a few minutes she put it down and found herself staring off at nothing in particular. Martha finished the dishes and came from the kitchen, drying her hands with an apron. She looked at Valerie and the book closed upon her lap, and she came up beside her, laying a hand upon her daughter's shoulder.

"This has been a terrible day, darling."

Valerie patted her mother's hand. "I'm all right, Mother. I was just thinking."

"About Joe?"

Valerie nodded her head. She had been thinking of Joe Lascoe . . . and other things.

"Joe was with us a long time. We grew to depend on that man. I'll miss him almost as much as I miss your father." Martha's voice hardened. "I hope Jenney finds that Hank Acker and whoever else was in on the doing of this thing and strings them up!"

Valerie frowned. "Killing only leads to more killing, Mother."

Martha nodded wearily. "I know, child. That's the way of things out here."

Valerie started to speak, changed her mind, and looked at the closed book upon her lap. It was Dickens's *Great Expectations.*

Martha noted the movement. "You miss it, don't you?"

Valerie raised an eyebrow.

"The East. You miss it, don't you?"

"Yes, I miss it, Mother."

"Honey, this is your home. It's where you belong."

"Is it?" Valerie was suddenly irritated. "Why do I belong here, Mother? Because I'm an Indian? The Indians don't claim me. Whoever heard of an Indian with a college degree in English literature? And the white men don't want me as one of their own either! College degree or not, I'm still a squaw in their eyes. No, Mother, all I have is you and one or two of the older ranch hands who have known me all my life. Now that Joe is dead, I guess that amounts to just you and Dave Thompson. No, Mother, I don't belong here at all!"

"But someday the Largo will be yours."

"And what am I to do with it? You helped Father build the Largo, but now that he's gone, it's even too much for you to handle. How could I ever expect to turn it into anything?"

"Someday you'll marry, darling, then you'll have a man to help you."

"Yes, someday I will marry, but it won't be a man from Esteros Creek."

Martha must have seen it in her daughter's eyes, for all at once she understood what had been tormenting Valerie since her return home. "There is someone already. Someone back east."

Valerie looked away and nodded.

"What's his name?"

"What difference does it make? He's in New York and I'm in New Mexico."

"He can come out. Dave could teach him about ranching in no time!"

"Come out *here*!" Valerie said in mild disbelief. "Why would he want to come out here?" She lifted the book from her lap. "He'd sooner move to Charles Dickens's

England than Valerie Kincade's New Mexico! And to be truthful, I would too."

Martha's eyes welled up, and she looked away. "Your father and I, we tried to give you a good life. . . ."

"Oh, Mother," Valerie said, going to her mother's side, at once feeling wicked and terribly ungrateful. "It's not your fault. It's not anyone's fault. I do appreciate all you and Father have done for me, but I really don't belong here anymore."

"What are you going to do, then?"

"Do," Valerie said thoughtfully. "Why, I'm going to stay right here and help you as best I can. Someday, when the ranch is back on its feet and I know you're in a good position again, well, then perhaps I'll return to the East and find a job. I could become a teacher."

"And your young man?"

Valerie moved to the window, turning her back to Martha. "The East is full of men," she said, "good men —I'll find another." She tried to hide the catch in her voice. The front door swung open just then, and Manuel burst in, his brown eyes wide.

"Señora, the men, they return from town!" he said.

From the bay window Valerie watched the carriage roll under the adobe portals and up to the house. Dave Thompson turned his horse in at the hitching rail, and Edgar and Billy continued on to the bunkhouse.

Dave climbed the stairs and removed his hat as he came through the door. "How are you feeling, ma'am?" he said to Martha.

"I have had better days, Dave, but I will be all right."

He looked at Valerie. "You okay, Val?"

"Like Mother, I'll be all right."

"How'd it go in town? What did Jenney have to say?" Martha wanted to know.

Dave grimaced. "We took care of all that needed tending. Burt wants to see Valerie in the morning."

"Me?" Valerie stepped away from the window.

"Yes, ma'am. He wants to hear your version of the incident. He's reluctant to take Bracken's word on it." Dave frowned. "Burt seems to think Thomas might be using this to settle up a score between himself and Acker."

"A score? That's ridiculous!" she bristled.

"Yes, ma'am, I know that, but just the same, I agreed to bring you into town tomorrow morning."

It was pointless to get angry. She relaxed, and folded her hands in front of her dress. "Okay, Dave," she said, "I'll go into town with you tomorrow."

"I have some coffee on," Martha said. "Stay for a cup?"

"Yes, ma'am," he said, almost as if he knew it was coming.

Valerie watched the two of them disappear into the kitchen. Like Dave, she too understood the unspoken meaning in that invitation, and it had nothing to do with Martha being a perfect hostess.

18

Dave knew that when Martha offered him coffee in that tone of voice, she had something on her mind other than being cordial. Generally it had to do with ranch business, especially when she was worried about something. Lately he had been taking a lot of coffee up at the house.

She filled two cups and sat at the table across from him, wrapping her pale hands around the warm china. "Dave," she started when he set down his cup and leaned back in his chair, "how is the herd doing?"

"Those animals are fattening up real fine, ma'am. I have 'em grazing that tall grass down along the Old River. Yesterday I sent a couple boys on a gather up to the plateau. They'll be driving what they find down to the valley to fatten up with the rest."

"Do we have enough animals—enough to make our payments, I mean?" Martha lowered her voice so that her words wouldn't be heard in the next room. "I'm worried, Dave, if we have another bad year, I stand a chance of losing the Largo!"

She paused, studied his face, then glanced away and contemplated the coffee in her cup. "I've got another farmer wanting to put in cotton along the Porter," she said, sounding almost embarrassed by it. Her voice was strained. "I don't want to sell, but if we come up short again this year . . . well, losing a few hundred acres is better than losing the whole ranch."

Dave frowned. Like the other cowmen in the valley, he didn't regard with favor selling off good ranch land to the sod busters, but he didn't want the Largo to fall into the hands of the bank either. He was keenly aware of Martha's dilemma.

"We have us a good herd this year. After we drive 'em to the railhead and pay off the drovers, I figure you'll clear about six thousand—or thereabouts. I don't know what all you owe the bank. Will that be enough to keep us going till next year?"

Martha's tight-lipped expression eased into more gentle lines, and she said, "Yes, Dave, six thousand will get us through the year."

"Then if that's the amount you need, that's what I'll get for you. Tomorrow morning I'll send another three or four men to help gather down south and keep an eye on the animals along the river."

"I know you have been working shorthanded," Martha said. "Maybe next year we can hire on a couple more men. I want to get this ranch producing again, like it was when Jim was running it."

Dave leaned back in his chair and discovered he was

smiling. "That was the prime of life, wasn't it? We had us quite a spread. . . ."

Martha's lips twisted suddenly. Her breath caught in her throat and choked off the smile that had spread over her face. She clutched her left shoulder and trembled. Dave came out of his chair.

"What is it?"

She waved him back. "Sit down, Dave, sit down. I'm all right," she said between short, painful breaths. "I'm all right."

"Twinges again?"

Martha nodded her head and motioned him back to the chair. He was reluctant, but Martha insisted. She wheezed with each breath and after a few minutes began to breathe more easily again. The tortured look on her face relaxed, and she brought her trembling hands back to the table. "They pass after a moment."

"You haven't been looking well these last few days," Dave said, concerned. "And those pains seem to have become worse now than just twinges. You're white as a ghost. Maybe you should go talk with Doc Lester."

"I have. He told me I have to slow down and take it easy. I haven't got time to take it easy, Dave. I'm going to build this spread back to what it used to be! We've weathered our share of hard times since Jim left, but times are getting better, I can feel it."

"Mother?" Valerie's voice came from the parlor. Then her face appeared in the kitchen doorway. "Someone's coming up the road, and he's riding real hard!"

Dave pushed back from the table and crossed the parlor to the door. Valerie returned to the large bay window as the rider came up the dark road on a fast horse and reined in at the house.

"That's Mr. Bracken," Valerie said. "What's he doing out here tonight?"

Dave Thompson was already down by the hitching rail. The two men talked, and in a moment Dave spun away and sprinted across the gray moonlit compound, into the shadows of the bunkhouse. Langely wrapped his reins around the hitching rail and climbed the steps to the porch.

Valerie met him at the door. "Mr. Bracken?"

He looked from her to Martha and said, "Mrs. Kincade, Dave went to round up some men. I'm afraid trouble is coming your way."

Martha's lips thinned. Her eyes hardened. "What kind of trouble?"

There was no easy way to tell it. He glanced at Valerie's astonished face, then back at Martha. "I learned from one of the Double T hands that Hank Acker and some of his friends are planning to blow up the dam in Porter Canyon tonight."

"My God!" Martha stumbled back as if his words had been a fist. "Our cattle! All our cattle are grazing in the river valley!"

"Dave told me."

"We've got to stop them!" Valerie said.

"I rode out as soon as I learned."

Martha groped for the arm of a nearby chair and lowered herself into it.

"Why are they doing this to us? Why does the Double T hate us so?" Valerie demanded. "The fight between our two ranches has been over for years. Why can't they leave us alone?"

"I don't think the Double T is behind this."

"But you just said—"

"I said they were Double T hands, I didn't say they were working under orders of Thaddeus Tyrell."

"I don't understand—who, then?"

"I don't know yet. The man doing the talking died before I could get it out of him." Langely had his growing suspicions, but that was all they were—suspicions, and no proof.

"Died?" Valerie regarded the gun on his hip. Her black eyes peered up into his face, intent, her voice cautious. "Who was he?"

"The name I heard was Canon."

"Albert Canon," she said, shifting her view from his face to stare into space. "Well, I'm sure he deserved it," she said all at once. "He must of had a hand in this terrible scheme!"

"Probably," Langely said. The sound of horses out front drew his attention. Dave Thompson came up the steps.

Martha looked up from the chair with the tortured, colorless face of a woman whose world was crumbling all around her and there was little she could do about it.

"Thomas tell you?"

She nodded her gray head.

"We'll be going, then."

"Be careful," was all Martha could say.

Valerie stood in the window as the two men swung into their saddles and the riders spurred their horses out onto the south road.

Then she turned slowly away from the window and crossed the wide room. Except for Martha's heavy, raspy breathing, terrifying silence had suddenly settled around them. "Everything will work out, Mother," she said, putting a consoling hand on her mother's shoulder. "Dave and Mr. Bracken will take care of it," she said, trying not to betray her real fears.

19

Dave Thompson moved into the lead once out on the south road, and a mile from the house he swung off of it onto a trail that snaked back into the dark hills. They rode quickly. A nearly full moon made travel easy, and their horses kept up the pounding pace until the hills closed in around them.

Earlier that morning at the river crossing, Valerie had told him the ranch house was eleven miles away. But the nature of a river being what it is, twisting and turning through valleys and deep arroyos, the dam could lie almost anywhere among the dark and tortured chasms that etched this high desert landscape. To find it on his own would have required Langely to retrace his tracks to the cottonwood forest and then follow the banks of the shallow rill up into Porter Canyon to the place between the narrows where Jim Kincade had built his dam. It would have cost valuable minutes—minutes now being eaten away as their horses galloped across the shadowy landscape.

The minutes turned into a score of minutes, and then forty before Dave raised a hand and brought them to a halt atop a ridge overlooking a wide valley. Below lay the broad, empty banks of the Porter. Although twenty years had passed, Langely could still see the signs that told him that at one time these empty banks had contained the waters of a swift river. Tall trees marched alongside the wedge-shaped course cut deep into the valley floor, and a sea of cattle spread out along the empty riverbed, grazing contentedly.

At first sight the cattle standing among the tall grass in the pale light of the moon had a certain pastoral peacefulness about them—a picture quickly shattered when Langely reminded himself of the circumstances that had brought him to this spot.

Dave leaned back in his saddle. "Well, we aren't too late yet," he said. "Billy, ride down there and find our men. Get 'em the hell out of that valley. Then circle around to the ridge and haze off to the south rim of the canyon. Keep an eye out. The rest of us will head for the north rim and meet you at the dam. If you see anyone or anything that looks out of place, especially if it happens to be hauling dynamite, shoot it!"

Edgar stood in his stirrups and motioned toward a stand of cottonwood trees growing up at the mouth of the canyon. "Looky, Dave, down yonder. Ain't that a campfire I see flickering?"

Dave bent forward to study the far-off point of light and nodded his head. "That's our men. Billy, get 'em out of there."

"That's one hell of an unfortunate spot to be camping

if the dam should bust loose," Bill Tremely observed as he nudged his horse onto a trail.

As Billy started down the steep descent, Dave Thompson turned to the waiting men. His face was grave, and nothing further needed to be said. He kneed his mount onto another trail and started down it.

The single low boom that echoed in the night sounded far away, and almost harmless at first as it rose from somewhere deep within the valley. A mile to the east an orange glow spread above the dark hills and faded quickly against the blacker landscape, and then a distant rumbling, like the approach of a hundred freight trains, rolled out of the canyon. Without warning, the stillness of the night was rocked. Langely's horse threw back its head and sidestepped into a piñon tree. He tugged at the reins, and the earth began to tremble beneath them.

The cattle were stirred into nervous circles in the valley below as the ground groaned and the freight trains steamed nearer to the mouth of the long tunnel. All at once the cows sparked into a stampede. Langely watched the grim scene unfold, scarcely aware of the men around him, conscious only of the frantic glut of cattle funneling out of the valley by way of the dried riverbed.

Bill Tremely's horse pounded back up the trail and spun to a halt. "Did you see it?" he was shouting, "Did you see that explosion!"

The cattle were clamoring down the valley when the thirty-foot-high wall of water burst from the mouth of Porter Canyon.

* * *

The terrified cries of dying cattle ceased almost at once as the water pounded from the narrow confines of the canyon and filled the valley. Uprooted trees disappeared with the torrent that split wide the breach in the dam. The suddenly freed water spread out across the valley, rose up the walls, and then retreated back to the inundated river channel and rushed away, washing clean all life.

The earth ceased to tremble, and the Largo herd—all but for a fortunate few that had managed to climb to higher ground—was gone. The night grew strangely silent, a silence heightened by desultory cries of the scattered animals that remained alive.

The riders sat helpless as the devastation unfolded below them, and when it was over, Dave turned his horse off the ridge and started down into the valley. One by one the men followed. Langely lingered a moment after they had gone and let his eyes sweep along the river valley. Nothing remained. The knee-high grass had been flattened by the water. The cottonwood trees at the mouth of the canyon, the first to be ripped from the ground as the river burst free, were nowhere to be found. And the men? Three had been camped with the herd. Had any escaped, or had they been carried away too?

He started his horse into the valley after the last man had descended from the ridge top. A hundred yards from the river his horse splashed into water and matted grass. Dave raised a hand, halting the line of men, and moved his gaze up and down the long valley. He wasn't seeing only the loss of cattle and three men, Langely knew. Dave Thompson was seeing the end of the Largo.

"The men who did this are long gone by now." Dave

spoke in a low voice, empty of emotion. "The best we can do is salvage what's left. Billy, you and Edgar see if you can find any traces of our boys on the face of the canyon. They may have had time to climb to higher ground before the water hit.

"John . . . Larry, head east and bring what's left of the herd back here." Dave looked at Langely. "We'll go west, along the river. Roger, you come with us.

"Look for cattle that might be hurt, or just trapped in muddy places. If they can be helped, do so. If they are beyond it, put them out of their pain. Keep count of the dead best you can."

He glanced at Langely. "Did you ever work cattle, Mr. Bracken?"

"No."

"Well, you're going to get a whole bellyful of learning tonight."

It was daylight when the men came back up the river. They returned singly, or in pairs, dead tired in their saddles. They had found dead cows as far west as the cottonwood forest by the road and had managed to gather in most that hadn't drowned. They had pulled animals from the mud and freed them from entanglements of trees and shrubs. Those beasts beyond help had been shot—until bullets ran out—and when the ammunition was gone, the injured had been left bellowing in pain to wait for their wounds, or the coyotes, to kill them.

When the count was in, three hundred and forty-three animals remained alive out of the more than a thousand that had been swept away.

"We have maybe another hundred and fifty head to

the north," Dave said, "and a couple hundred down by the ranch—perhaps six hundred in all, counting those we saved tonight."

He asked Bill Tremely if he had found any trace of the men. Bill said no. Dave shook his head slowly and drew in a long breath. He said to Roger, "Ride out to the line shack and tell our men there what happened. Have them drive the cattle on the plateau down here to the valley, where the grass is still plentiful."

Roger rode off, and Dave told the rest of the men to stay with the cattle, finally turning to Langely. "Ain't much more we can do here."

With the weight of what had happened this night pressing their spirits, Langely and Thompson turned their horses away from the valley and rode back to give the grim news to Martha Kincade.

20

They rode under the adobe portals and dismounted at the bunkhouse. Dave Thompson wrapped his reins around the hitching rail and came around the back of his horse. "Can you stay around for a while, Bracken?" he asked.

Langely nodded his head at the saddlebags tied behind his saddle. "Everything I own is there. No reason why I can't stay, and besides, there's a sheriff back in town who is probably real anxious to see me behind bars."

"Jenney? What did you do this time to rile Burt?"

Langely shrugged his shoulders and slackened the cinches on the saddle. "I locked him in one of his own cells."

Dave permitted one of his rare grins to crease his face.

"The sheriff wasn't about to let me ride out of town

last night, and I could not think of any other peaceable way to convince him."

Dave shook his head, and there was a genuine smile now in place of the grin. "Go inside and pick yourself a bed." His voice turned somber. "We've got plenty of empties to choose from."

"A bed sounds mighty inviting at the moment. Thanks."

"There's a stock of cartridges in the supply cabinet inside. Take what you need. After all, you spent all yours on ranch business." A shadow moved across Dave's face. "Well, I'd better go tell the Kincades." He left the horses and crossed the compound to the house. Langely didn't envy him for what he had to do.

Valerie came out onto the porch as Dave climbed the steps. She was wearing a simple yellow dress with ruffles around the neck. A pretty dress that for some reason reminded Langely of Sarah.

He put the thought aside, turned their horses loose in the corral, and carried his rifle and saddlebags inside. The bunkhouse was indeed man-poor and bed-rich. He found the bullets where Dave said they would be, loaded his revolver, and filled the empty loops of his cartridge belt. Then he fell onto a bunk that appeared unused and kicked off his boots. Old habits die hard, and now that he had started to carry a revolver again, he found himself arranging the holster on the mattress so that the grip of the weapon fell close to hand. Outside, the noon sun baked down on the bunkhouse roof and glared through the dingy glass windows. He tugged his hat over his eyes and immediately was asleep.

* * *

Martha Kincade gripped the arm of the chair as if it were a lifeline thrown out from a passing ship . . . as if she had no strength of her own left to rely upon. Her ashen hands and bony knuckles were white against the polished wood.

"I left the boys with the cows we managed to save," Dave said, fingering the brim of his hat in his hands. "I'm hoping we'll find some more, but they're probably scattered from hell and gone by this time."

He wasn't sure she had heard him. Martha appeared to be watching something suspended between the ceiling and the floor. Something only she could see. Thompson cleared his throat and said, "As soon as we can spare an extra man, I'll send someone into town to tell Burt."

"Ransing and Kelterman, they have kin somewhere," Martha said then, her eyes remaining fixed on that unseen something suspended above the floor. "We'll need to locate their families and tell them. I don't know about Franklin." She glanced up. "You ever hear Solly Franklin talk about family?"

"No, but I'll ask the men. Perhaps they know if he had somebody who ought to be notified."

At this moment Martha seemed frail, small—almost swallowed by the chair she had fallen into when Dave brought the word of their losses, both of men and of animals. Valerie had stepped silently up beside her and gripped her mother's shoulders with strong fingers.

"Someone ought to ride out to the farmers that bought land along the river and see if any were harmed by the water."

Dave pulled his eyes off of Martha and looked at Valerie. "Yes, ma'am. I was planning to do that just as soon as we freed up some men. Those farmers all have their homes on the high ground above the river. I suspect none of them was hurt, though we did see plenty of crop damage as we worked last night."

He looked back at Martha. She had resumed her vacant stare into space. "Well, ma'am, I've my day cut out for me. I'll stop in later and see how you're doing."

Valerie accompanied him to the door. Outside she put a hand on his arm and stopped him. "How bad is it, Dave, really?"

"It couldn't be much worse, Val," he said, looking down at her from beneath his wide hat. She seemed to bear up well, and if anything, had become stronger and more determined with the news. In that he saw a bit of Big Jim Kincade. Jim had been a fighter, and if he were alive now, he'd be strapping on a gun and riding out to find the men responsible for this. But that man—and maybe even those days—were gone. They'd have to let the law handle it—Burt Jenney—but the way he'd been acting lately . . .

"Is there anything I can do, Dave?"

Her question brought him back to the moment. "No. I'll take care of what needs doing. You stay near your mother. She needs you now. She could do with a little of your strength."

Valerie smiled, but there was no depth to it. "I will."

Dave Thompson went down the steps and angled toward the barn.

Thomas Langely woke some hours later, still tired. Long, hazy shafts of sunlight filtered through the low west windows. During the afternoon the men Dave had left at the river valley had returned. Their muffled snores and the loud, steady ticking of a clock on the wall were all that disturbed the late-afternoon stillness. He rolled out of bed and sat on the edge, rubbing his eyes. His body ached and pleaded for more sleep, but his stomach protested, aroused by the aroma of cooking food drifting down from the house.

He slung the gun belt over his shoulder and stepped outside, where a huge red sun hung low above the western hills, about to take the failing daylight elsewhere. Clouds were gathering on the eastern rim of the world, and a cool breeze came across the compound to snatch away the powder-fine dust kicked up by his boots as he walked. He marveled that he managed to sleep through the hot part of the afternoon. He must have been totally exhausted for that to happen. It had been his only sleep in thirty hours, and he longed to stumble back into bed and sleep another ten, but the aroma of steaks over a fire and baking potatoes pulled him to the house.

A dusty, one-horse buggy was tied in front at the hitching rail. The paint was scratched in spots, but the leather seat, although cracked and faded, was carefully mended in half a dozen different places where the seams had separated or the leather split. He eyed the buggy and went up the steps, wrapping a hand around the revolver still in its holster. At the door low voices reached his ears. He loosened the pistol in the leather and came through the door.

Sarah Lawrence and Valerie both looked up from the sofa, and their conversation trailed off. But for the two of them the room was empty.

"Sarah?" he said, feeling suddenly ridiculous holding the revolver. He relaxed and slipped the holster belt back to his shoulder.

"Sarah drove all the way out here to see you, Thomas," Valerie said. "We've been waiting for you to wake up. I was about to send Dave over to see if you were all right." She smiled. "Are you hungry?"

"Starving," he said. His eyes seemed unable to move off of Sarah.

"I'll go set an extra plate. Father used to say, 'A working man that claims he isn't hungry is either sick or a liar.' " Valerie got up, and as she passed, she said, "I'm glad that you're neither, *Mr. Bracken*," and she went to the kitchen.

"Thomas—" Sarah said coming to her feet.

"Why did you come here?"

"Oh, Thomas, you stirred up a real hornets' nest last night."

"Because of Canon?"

"I told Burt the whole story, how he . . . he attacked me like he did." Sarah lowered her eyes toward her long gray skirt.

Langely lifted her chin with a finger. "Did he believe you?"

"Oh, yes," she said quickly. "He understands that, but . . ."

"He's mad because I locked him in jail."

"I think that must be what's gotten into him, because I don't understand why he's acting like he is."

"He'll get over it. The only thing hurt was his pride."

She shook her head. A curl of golden hair fell across her eye, and she combed it away with a finger. "I don't think so. After you rode away last night, the whole town heard him calling from the side window of the jail. Someone found the keys, and when they unlocked him, he went fuming about town, and I don't know what he was looking for, but later he arrested Mr. Lemont!"

"Marcus? He didn't have anything to do with it. If anything, he took the sheriff's side!"

"I know, but like I said, Burt is not acting himself. I think he would have thrown *me* in jail too if I hadn't been a woman *and* the injured party."

Langely strode across the floor and turned sharply. "Marcus Lemont in jail. I don't understand it. Why him? Why not Edwin? He was standing there too. How can Jenney hold Lemont responsible for something I did, unless"—he came to a halt—"unless Jenney was afraid of what Lemont might find if he started digging through that pile of old newspapers."

Sarah frowned. "I don't know what you are talking about," she said, confused. "What did you mean when you told Mr. Lemont he should look into those old newspapers from the time Mr. Kincade was killed?"

"I was shooting in the dark"—he paused thoughtfully —"but it looks as if I may have hit something."

She shook her head as if to free her brain of the confusion. "I don't know what you're talking about, and I don't understand why you're being so mysterious."

"I'm not sure myself, Sarah."

She dismissed the subject with a wave of her hand and said, "That's not all. The sheriff has been rounding up men all morning for a posse. He knows who you are, the whole town knows." She paused to let the full impact of her words sink in.

Langely shook his head. "This is what I wanted to avoid," he said quietly. "It's why I changed my name. I was hoping to find a town where I could bury my past and build a new future. I was a fool to think that could ever be."

"Darling," she said suddenly, "we can still have that life, maybe not here in Esteros Creek, but somewhere." She flushed, embarrassed by her boldness. Now that it was said, he could either accept or reject her open heart.

Her words stunned him. Sarah was cutting herself in for more trouble than she knew. Was it fair of him to allow her to do that?"

Sarah's blue eyes suddenly widened. "You can't stay here. The sheriff and his posse might come anytime!"

If it wasn't for Sarah, and the killing of Joe Lascoe, he could saddle up and find another town, maybe over in Arizona. He didn't want to bring any more trouble to the doorsteps of the Largo, but he had already made too many ties here to simply ride away from it all. Leaving was no longer the simple matter of saddling up his horse.

He gave Sarah a wry smile. "You're right, I can't stay, but I'm not leaving until I get some of that food Valerie promised," he said, wanting to relieve some of the intense gloom that had settled over them. He took Sarah by the hand to the dining room, where Valerie was arranging knives and forks on the table.

"I was about to call, but didn't want to interrupt anything." She gave Sarah a wink. "You two sit down. Care for some coffee, Thomas?"

"Please."

"Sarah?"

"Oh, no thank you, Val."

"Tea, then?"

"Yes, I'll have some tea."

Valerie said, "Well, I'm going to have coffee. Father was a coffee man, the stronger the better, and he raised his daughter—to the frustration of his wife—to be a coffee drinker too."

Langely was suddenly aware of Martha's absence. "Where is your mother?"

"Mother went to bed early. She was very upset. First it was Joe, then the three men last night, not to mention losing the herd like that. She made herself ill thinking about it. I told her to go to bed. She'll be herself in a few days."

"What are you going to do now?" he asked.

"Do?" Her eyebrows raised with the question.

"You've lost most of the herd, and from what I understand, you're already head over heels in debt."

She shook her head. The dark expression added years to the young face. "I don't know what we are going to do, Mr. Brack—er, Thomas. If we lose the Largo, it will kill Mother."

"Is there much chance of that happening?" He sipped the coffee she had poured into his cup.

"Mr. Caldwell holds a number of loans Mother had to take to keep us from going under during these hard times. He has been very patient, but now I just don't know. Mother is behind on her payments." She shook her head again. "Yes, there is a good chance that we could lose it."

"Speaking of Caldwell," Sarah said, looking at Thomas, "my room at the hotel was on the northeast side, and I had a good view of the town last night. After Burt took Lemont to jail, I watched him go up to Mr. Caldwell's apartment. He lives on the second floor above the bank. It was late, but the door opened immediately when Burt knocked—almost as if Mr. Caldwell were expecting him. That struck me as being strange." Sarah's eyes clouded, and she bit down on her lip.

"I saw Jenney going up to Caldwell's place yesterday morning," Langely said.

Dave Thompson came into the kitchen from a back door, removed his hat, and gave the women a brief nod. He said to Langely, "Did Sarah tell you?"

"About the posse Jenney is rounding up?"

Dave straddled a chair, and Valerie poured him a cup of coffee. "I think it might be wise if you're not around when Jenney comes looking—"

"Sarah seems to share your opinion," he said.

"We have an old line shack about twelve miles north of here. Don't use it much anymore, what with the fewer men we've had. It's in the mountains, secluded—you'll be safe there. Spend a week or two till this trouble blows over."

"And then what?"

Dave shrugged. "Come back here if you like. We'll put you to work as long as we can hold on to this spread —now that most the cattle is gone. Won't be able to pay more than three squares a day, but at least it's a roof over your head. Or you can head out as you please. I just want you to know you're welcome to stay."

Langely sipped his coffee thoughtfully. It wasn't in his nature to run, and he certainly didn't intend to spend a week in hiding, but for the moment he needed someplace safe while he sorted out his thoughts. He'd suddenly acquired a lot to think about. He glanced at Sarah. Her eyes had widened hopefully. "All right," he agreed, "it's better than an out-and-out showdown in front of the house. How do I find the place?"

"I'll take you," Dave said, putting down his coffee cup and standing. "I'll have one of the boys saddle your horse and bring it around to the house. As soon as you finish eating, we'll leave. No telling how near Burt Jenney might be."

Dave hurried out the back door. Sarah gave Langely's arm a squeeze. "It won't be for very long. Everything will settle down in a day or two, and in a few weeks it will all be forgotten."

Her face brightened. He wanted to smile at her innocence, to hold her and protect her from the *real* world outside—but all he could give her was a grim frown.

21

Black clouds tumbled across angry skies, stealing the moonlight from above the seven horsemen as they rode into the compound and reined to a stop next to Sarah's buggy. To the east, electricity arced between heaven and earth, illuminating the small details of the tumult overhead as if caught in a photographer's flash. Jenney studied Sarah's open carriage, then cast a suspicious eye at the house, where drawn curtains glowed a warm amber.

"You boys wait here for me," he said, and went up the steps.

Valerie opened the door at his knock. "Why, Sheriff, what ever are you doing here at this late hour?" she said in a surprised voice. Her eyelids came together then. "Have you come to tell us that you have captured the men responsible for killing Joe?"

"You know why I'm here, Miss Kincade. May I come in?"

Valerie looked at the six men out front, then pulled the door wider and stepped back. Sarah was sitting in one of the large leather chairs when he came in. She peered at him over the cup of tea she was sipping and set it back on a saucer upon her lap.

"Miss Lawrence," Burt said, respectfully. "I'm not surprised to find you here. I suggest you have one of the ranch hands move your buggy to the barn. It looks like we are in for quite a storm."

"Thank you, Sheriff," Sarah said evenly, "I'll see to it."

Jenney turned to Valerie. "I've come for Thomas Langely. You'll make my job a whole lot easier if you just tell me where he is."

"He's not here, Sheriff."

"Miss Kincade," Burt started in a voice patently indulgent, "I know that Thomas Langely rode out here last night."

"That is correct. He came to warn us"—her words trailed off—"but he was too late." She was silent a moment, then fire flamed in her dark eyes. "Sheriff, why aren't you out after the men who killed Joe, the same rogues who blew up our dam last night, drowned our cattle, and killed three of our men?" she said hotly. "You know Hank Acker was involved in both these tragedies. Why isn't he behind bars?"

Jenney's face showed astonishment. "The dam was blown up?"

"We have been a little too busy to come in and report the incident to you formally, but surely you must have had some idea when you crossed the Porter River on your way here and saw that it was full of water—for the first time in twenty years!"

"Well, yes, I guess I did kind of wonder about that. What makes you think Hank Acker had anything to do with it?"

"What makes me think that? Albert Canon. He talked before he died. He told Thomas everything!"

Burt stiffened, and studied the young woman standing before him. He glanced across the room to Sarah Lawrence, then cleared his throat and asked, "Did Canon say who was behind it?"

"Unfortunately no." Valerie let her disappointment show. "He died before Thomas could get that out of him."

Burt pulled himself up tall and said, "I'll see to Acker, but right now I'm after Langely."

"Because he bested you in public?" Valerie said lightly.

Jenney's neck reddened. "He took the law into his own hands. He obstructed justice. I warned him!"

Sarah sprang from her chair. "You know what happened last night," she said angrily. "Thomas saved me from—from that awful man. Canon had a gun and he used it. Thomas killed in self-defense! But it's not because Thomas took the law into his own hands that's got you all fired up. It's because he made you look foolish in front of Mr. Lemont, and Edwin, and me. And then he locked you behind your own bars!" Sarah drew a ragged breath. "Thomas is not wanted here or anywhere else," she continued. "There are no warrants out on him, and you have no reason but your own vengeful pride to arrest him! Go after the real criminals."

Jenney weathered the brunt of Sarah's stormy attack, and when it subsided, he looked back at Valerie and said, "I'm sorry about Joe. We were friends, and I'm going to miss him. And it's regrettable about the cattle."

"And the three men who were killed too," Valerie reminded him.

Jenney frowned. "Who were they?"

"What difference does it make, Sheriff. You're only interested in one man, who stepped on your toes in front of a couple of witnesses—because of your own bullheadedness, I might add. Since your pride is obviously more important than the three men we lost, why should you care who they were?"

Jenney's neck turned a darker hue in the lamplight. "Miss Kincade, I will see to Hank Acker, I can promise you that. But right now I have come for Langely and I don't intend to leave without him."

"Then you have a long wait ahead of you, and you are not welcome to do it on my doorstep. He isn't here. He was here last night, but he knew you would be coming after him, so he left. Good night, Sheriff."

Jenney hesitated in the doorway, studying Valerie's dark eyes. She made a quick, careless gesture toward the parlor. "All right, go ahead and search the place if you want to, although it will be a waste of time better spent out running down Hank Acker."

Jenney glanced around the room, then out the door at his men waiting by their horses, busy shaking out their rain slickers and pulling them on. A jagged edge of light lit up the dark sky, and a distant rumble rolled up the valley. Jenney knew that if Thomas Langely was still on the ranch, he'd be well hidden by this time, and considering her willingness to let him search the place, Jenney suspected Valerie was telling him the truth. "You're probably right, ma'am, I don't expect I'll find him here," he said. "I don't suppose you know where he went?"

"He could be anywhere," she said.

He nodded curtly to the women and stepped back outside into the chill wind whipping in from the east.

"Don't forget Hank Acker," Valerie said.

Jenney paused on the steps and turned back toward the woman framed in the doorway of the big house to respond to that, then reconsidered and went down to his horse. Sarah's face appeared in the lighted doorway as Jenney untied his slicker from the back of the saddle and crawled into it. The posse mounted up and rode away into the impending storm.

22

Ahead the dark sky filled with stars as the night grew cool. Behind, a churning sea of black clouds tumbled after the two riders, sweeping away stars and obscuring all but the faintest glow of the moon. In an hour fat drops began to pelt the parched earth. They hunched down under their rain slickers and broad hats and continued on through the storm.

Lightning hurled jagged white lances to the earth, and with each rumble the horses recoiled nervously. Blinding flashes showed the landscape rising around them, growing rocky. Thomas Langely and the Largo foreman rode on through the storm that raged about them. Soon pine trees rose up alongside the trail. Their horses kicked and scraped along a steep, rocky path, climbing the shelf of a low mountain range. Sometime later Dave reined in and dismounted under a leaky log lean-to barn.

They unsaddled and hauled their gear along a soggy path to a dark cabin. Dave kicked the door open. Inside, Langely shut it against the storm while Dave struck a match and found a dusty oil lamp. Its untrimmed wick sputtered and burned poorly, grudgingly giving them light to work by. In a few minutes the two men were out of their slickers and had a second lamp trimmed and burning bright.

The previous occupants had been thoughtful enough to lay in a stack of dry tinder by the fireplace. Thomas started a fire to warm the room and dry out their clothes. Dave busied himself pulling open drawers and checking cabinets. He found a dusty bottle of whiskey on one of the shelves and set it on the table. A stack of tin plates, a blue enameled coffeepot, and some tin cups were the only other items left in the cabin. Dave blew the dust off the coffeepot, which had been left on the stone ledge beside the fireplace, and crawled back into his slicker. A minute later he returned with the pot full of water.

"There's a water barrel out back, and a stream about twenty yards south of the cabin," he said as he hung the coffeepot over the fire and shed the dripping slicker. They swept out the cabin, dusted the table, and afterward sat down with warming cups of coffee in their hands.

The fire on the hearth, the hot coffee, and the dry roof over their heads soon drove the chill from their bodies, and they set about wiping the moisture from their revolvers.

Langely methodically broke down his revolver, drying each piece. As he worked, he asked Dave how long he had been with the Largo.

"A long time," Dave said, giving his own revolver a hasty once-over with a cloth and shoving it back into the wet holster. "I wasn't much more than a kid when Big Jim and Martha staked out the boundaries of the Largo. Jim hired me on and taught me the business. I stayed till the war, then joined up when the fighting broke out. Afterward I came back."

Langely reassembled his weapon, eying the fit of each piece as it went back together. Dave lazed back in the chair and toyed with his cup on the table, remembering. Langely said, "I understand Burt Jenney used to work for Jim Kincade too."

"Uh-huh," Dave grunted without looking up from his cup. "Burt started about the same time I did, but he never went away to fight in the war, and soon he had himself worked in as being Jim's right-hand man. I think Jim would have made Burt his foreman 'cept Joe Lascoe had the job at the time, and Joe was good."

"What made Burt quit?"

Dave frowned. "Him and Jim had a falling out about the time that range war broke out between the Largo and the Double T."

Dave rocked back in his chair, remembering. "You see, back around sixty-six Big Jim had hired on an Indian couple to help with the work around the house that Jim was building. They weren't Kiowa—those were the ones we were having most the trouble with—no, they were Pueblo, and a nicer couple you ain't never met. Big Jim found them in Santa Fe one spring when he took a string of wagons up for their supplies—Esteros Creek wasn't much of a town back then." Dave snickered. "Ain't much of a town now, when you come down to the truth of the matter.

"Well, he brought this Indian couple back to the Largo, and it was surprising how well they took to each other, considering that that was the same time the Largo and the Double T were joined up and fighting the Kiowa. It just goes to show, you can't judge one Indian by the other—or any other folks for that matter. Martha Kincade was always a tough woman, but she was fresh out of the East—she used to teach piano music, I was told—and in the early days still what you would call wet behind the ears. She didn't know beans about docterin' up wounded men, so when we carried Big Jim in with a Kiowa arrow in his back one day in the fall of sixty-seven, Martha was as helpless as a newborn pup. It was the Indian woman that doctored up her Jim, and from that day on they became fast friends."

Langely wiped the dust from the bottle of whiskey and filled two cups.

"After they resolved the Kiowa trouble, Mr. Tyrell and Big Jim began to bicker and quarrel amongst themselves. It had to do with the dam Jim was building. You see, the Porter River worked its way through the Largo down onto Double T land, and Mr. Tyrell didn't like the idea of having a source of water for his cattle dried up, even though he already had good water. The Rio Gallianas runs right down the middle of his land. Just the same, I can't say as I blame him. I'd be upset, too, if it was my water, but the main part of the Porter was on Largo land, and Jim felt he had a right to build that reservoir to ensure water for his herd during the dry summer months. Well, that was the start. Other things played into the picture, too, and one thing led to another until the countryside was embroiled in a bloody war. We lost a lot of good men—on both sides.

"During this time the Indian woman had a baby girl, and it wasn't long afterward both she and her husband were killed when the Double T made a raid on the house. Martha and Jim raised the girl as their own. Martha was barren, you see, and the Kincades had always wanted children. The child had an Indian name, but Martha went and changed it to Valerie. Valerie was Jim's mother's name, and I'll tell you, Thomas, that girl could not have been treated any better if she had been their own flesh and blood.

"All the while this was going on, Burt Jenney was thinking maybe he was entitled to a share of the ranch. He figured he'd earned it fighting the Indians, the Double T, and working like he did. But the Kincades saw it different.

"When Valerie turned five, the Kincades announced they were legally adopting the girl, and that was the match that lit Burt's fuse. So long as the Kincades had no family, Burt figured that one day, if he played his cards right, the ranch would be his. But now that Valerie was the heir, Jenney was out of the picture. It came down to a confrontation, and Big Jim kicked Burt off the ranch. Well, Burt moved into town, and a month or so later he was sheriff."

Langely sipped his whiskey, piecing together a picture of Esteros Creek's past from the handful of facts he'd gleaned from the barber and Dave. "How old was Valerie when Jim was killed?"

Dave's brows knitted together, and his lips moved, silently counting the years. "Well," he said after a long, introspective moment, "I guess she must have been ten or eleven at the time—yes, I think that's about right, because I remember Martha worrying over Jim making her little girl into a little boy, and that must have been when Val was about eleven. You see, Jim took her hunting and fishing, and in the mornings they'd have their coffee together, then ride out to check the cattle."

Dave chuckled. "Yep, Martha was fit to be tied the way Jim was raising up a son instead of a daughter. One day Jim and Val went into town for supplies, and when they returned, Valerie was wearing a brand-new pair of store-bought britches. Martha was horrified. Sent the girl straight to her room to put a proper dress on, then Martha laid into Big Jim right there on the porch in front of all the hands." Dave smiled and shook his head. "I can still hear Big Jim telling her that if Valerie was going to ride with him and work cattle, she was going to dress for it. Martha wouldn't hear of it, but the next morning Valerie rode off with her pa wearing them new store-bought britches."

Dave laughed and nodded his head with a far-off gleam in his eye. "Quite a pair, Martha and Jim were. Didn't often see them argue—'cept when it came to raising Valerie. Well, I can't blame Jim. He wanted a son to leave the ranch to, and instead he had a daughter, so he just naturally took to raising her as if she was a boy. And I can't blame Martha either. She was raised in the East with certain notions on how a girl was to act." Dave paused and looked at the tin cup in his hand.

"After Jim was killed, Martha tried her darndest to break Valerie of Jim's bad teachings, but she got to the girl too late. Oh, Valerie is quite a lady, don't get me wrong, but she still has her daddy's spunk. That girl can hold her own when it comes to a push comes to shove, just like her daddy."

Langely recalled Valerie squinting down the barrel of

her rifle at Hank Acker. If that was a little of Big Jim Kincade rubbing off, he would have liked to have met the man himself. He told Dave so.

Dave Thompson just grinned and settled back in his chair. He had a slew of stories to tell about Big Jim Kincade, and all night to tell them.

23

Edwin shivered in the morning chill on the sidewalk in front of the hotel. The rain had stopped falling sometime during the night, and high overhead the tattered remains of yesterday's black thunderclouds fled swiftly across the sky, playing a hide-and-seek game with the new sun. Edwin pushed out his chest, pulled the cool, clean morning air into his lungs, and with a look of vexation ventured out into the muddy street, where sticky clay sucked at his shoes. He climbed to the sidewalk across the street in front of Burt Jenney's office and diligently scraped his soles clean on the edge of a board.

Tipping his hat to two ladies strolling by, he offered a cheerful "Good morning" and expressed his delight at the fine rain Esteros Creek had gotten last night.

The ladies returned his cheeky smile and continued, chatting, up the street. Edwin stepped to the general store and tried the newly repaired door. It was locked? He tried the handle again, then rapped on the windowpane and peeked inside.

"Good morning, Edwin."

The voice at his back startled him. "Oh, Mr. Easterman! I didn't hear you come up."

"I should say not." Louis Easterman smiled. "You were quite intent at that window." Easterman was wearing a light-gray hat and a gray suit. His shoes were immaculate. He tucked his polished black strolling cane under his arm and bent for a peek in the window. Straightening, he turned a questioning eye toward Edwin.

"I was looking for Sarah," Edwin explained. "The store is still locked up. Usually it is open by this time." Edwin paused, then said, "Soap. The hotel is completely out of soap."

"And your patrons are complaining?" Easterman suggested.

Edwin frowned. "One," he said unhappily.

"There is always that *one*," Easterman said as if he understood all the troubles of the world.

Edwin rapped on the door again. "Miss Lawrence is never late. Do you happen to have the time?"

Easterman pulled a gold watch from his vest pocket and snapped open the case. "It's a quarter past eight."

Edwin wrung his hands and shook his head. "I just don't understand why Miss Lawrence is late. It's not like her, you know."

Easterman's brows drew an analytical crease above his dark eyes. "Perhaps with all the excitement this weekend she is still in her quarters?"

Edwin cast an eye at the gray sheets of clouds sweeping overhead. "The sky *is* much darker than usual. Do you suppose she overslept?"

"Perhaps," Easterman allowed, and glanced to rove along the storefront. "I think, though, that this establishment is becoming a bit much for Miss Lawrence to handle alone. I've offered to buy the business from her on numerous occasions. Offered more than the place is worth—but she refuses."

"Sarah is a stubborn woman," Edwin said, looking up into Easterman's angular, carefully barbered face. "Of course what would Sarah do if she didn't have the store? I mean, an unmarried girl has to earn a living." Edwin cleared his throat. "Er . . . a respectable living, that is."

"I'm in complete agreement," Easterman said quickly. "I've offered to buy her store for a respectable sum of money with the promise of a permanent job. I don't have the time to take from my law practice to see to the place properly, so Sarah would be a great help to me if she would stay on and run it. I, in turn, would be removing the burden of ownership. She could hire on help and be able to take a few days off when she wanted to."

Edwin sighed and bobbed his round, bald head. "That would be for the best, I feel. Sarah works so hard at this store. I often see lights burning late into the night."

Both men spent a silent moment on the sidewalk in front of the general store, wagging their heads in agreement. Then Easterman said, "I was just on my way to the La Casa Luna for breakfast. Since Miss Lawrence has not yet opened up, perhaps you would like to join me?"

"Thank you, Mr. Easterman, but I really must find Sarah and hurry back with the soap."

"Then might I suggest the rear door?" Easterman directed his walking stick up the narrow alley between the general store and Burt Jenney's office. "Just around the back. She lives there, you know."

"Yes, I know. I'll try. Thank you."

Easterman smiled, gave a curt bow from the waist, and walked his ebony stick to the café. Edwin bestowed a final rap upon the door. It remained closed. He abandoned the sidewalk and started down the narrow alleyway toward the rear of the building, walking the high edge where the mud was not so prevalent.

He came suddenly alert, stopping abruptly as the hushed words of two men talking in low voices reached his ears from behind the jailhouse.

". . . knows, yeah, Canon talked before he died!"

Edwin recognized Burt Jenney's subdued voice at once from the fragmented sentence. He thought at first to poke his head around and say hello, but the secretive tones stopped him, and he crept along the wall closer to the corner.

"How much does he know?" asked a voice Edwin did not recognize.

"Your guess is as good as mine," Jenney said. "According to the Indian girl, he isn't saying much, but he's starting to piece things together."

"The cat's out of the bag now."

"It better not be!" Jenney came back savagely. "If I go down, you're coming with me, understand?"

"Calm down, Burt. We've got to figure this thing out."

"Attacking Joe and the Kincade girl was a damn stupid move!" Burt said lowering his voice.

"I didn't hear any objections when we told you."

"You said you were going to have some fun. You didn't say anything about killing Joe Lascoe!"

"That was an accident."

"Accident, hell! Anytime you throw lead at people, you can expect an *accident* to happen, Acker!"

Hank Acker?

"Okay, so we got carried away—"

"And you botched the job last night too—killed three men!"

In the shadows between the two buildings Edwin's forehead creased.

"I warned you to be careful. I had it planned so we'd get the place without any bloodshed. Now the Largo is up in arms and hot for your hide. I'm sticking my neck out covering for you while that Montana *pistolero* is loose somewhere. I don't like it. Too many complications all of a sudden."

"You said Langely hightailed it out of here?"

"That's what *she* said. I don't believe her."

"Then we'll have to take care of him," Acker said.

"You leave him alone!" Jenney snapped. "If you hadn't picked a fight with him in the first place, we wouldn't have him breathing down our backs now."

"How was I supposed to know who he was. He wasn't wearing a gun. He came across like some no-account drifter."

"I had a feeling about that man the first time I laid eyes on him," Jenney said thoughtfully.

Edwin pressed closer to the adobe wall near the corner.

"Well, ain't nothing we can do about that now," Jenney said a little louder. "We've got to figure a way to cover our tracks while we yet have time, and still get our hands on the Largo."

"Okay"—Acker's words took on a more methodical pace—"first we find out who knows what, then we get rid of them."

Edwin conjured up a vision of Burt frowning as he heard the sheriff say, "That *pistolero* knows more than he's letting on. I don't know how he found out—but he did. Then there's Valerie Kincade and Sarah Lawrence. They're both getting suspicious. And Lemont—"

"Lemont? What does that old rummy know?"

"Too much if he starts digging through his old newspapers—" Jenney stopped abruptly, cleared his throat and said, "He just knows too much. I want him taken care of."

"That should be no problem. You still have him locked up, don't you?"

"He's inside, but it's got to look accidental. I don't want anybody snooping around my jail looking for answers. It's got to be done away from here!"

"I can handle that. Let Lemont go. That old gaffer has a reputation for tipping up a bottle. Everyone in town knows it. Tonight me and Lowe will pay him a visit. Pour some whiskey around and leave the empty bottle where someone will find it, then tip over a lamp. It'll look like Lemont got drunk and knocked the lamp over himself."

"I don't like having any more killings on our hands," Jenney said, "but we've got to cover our tracks while we're still able. From now on let's be particularly careful not to botch it!" he said, emphasizing the last phrase.

Edwin was becoming aware of the gravity of the words he was overhearing, and the grim consequences should Burt Jenney and Hank Acker catch him eaves-dropping. His hands began to shake, and suddenly he wanted to flee before they discovered him! Trembling, he pushed from the wall and backed down the long alley. His heel caught a jutting rock, and in a moment of panic to regain his balance, he tripped over his own feet and tumbled backward.

"What was that?" Jenney said, abandoning his secretive tone.

"The alley," Acker said.

They came around the corner as Edwin was scrambling to his feet. Burt grabbed hold of the little man. Acker contained his flailing arms, and they pulled him behind the jailhouse.

"You little snoop!" Acker growled. He slammed Edwin up against the building, held him there below his crisp new paper collar, and hauled back his fist. "I'll teach you to stick your nose where it don't belong!"

Burt grabbed Hank's arm and moved in front of the trembling, wide-eyed desk clerk. "How much did you hear, Edwin?"

"I . . . I didn't hear nothin', Sheriff," Edwin stammered, "I . . . I was just going back to see if Sarah was around . . . that's all." Edwin's wide eyes leaped from Acker to Jenney, then back again.

"He's lying." Acker's eyes compressed to two dark slits.

Jenney glanced at his accomplice. "What the hell do we do now?"

Acker grinned then. "What choice do we have?"

Jenney was silent a moment. "Tie him up and lock him in the back room. Tonight you and Lowe will take him along when you visit Lemont. It'll look natural enough. They're friends, aren't they?"

Edwin's face blanched. They hauled him through the back door, stuffed a rag in his mouth, lashed his hands, and deposited him on the closet floor with his knees tucked under his chin so that the door would close.

In the sudden darkness Edwin struggled uselessly against the rope that bound him. He could hear feet scrape the floor beyond the sliver of light beneath the door where shadows moved. Through the roar of pumping blood that swelled in his ears he heard Jenney's voice. "I'll go out front and release Lemont." The words were whispered, but oddly Edwin heard them as if they had been shouts in the darkness. "You get out of here and stay out of sight. I don't want anybody seeing you wandering around free and wondering why I haven't thrown you in jail."

"I'll be back after the sun goes down to pick up the little snoop." Acker's words came distinctly from beyond the other side of the closed closet door, as if he had moved down the hallway. "After we finish with them, we can start making arrangements for a couple of fatal accidents for the Lawrence girl and her high-and-mighty Indian friend."

"And don't forget Langely," Jenney said.

"You can't believe all those stories you hear. Anyway Lowe is pretty fair with a six-shooter, I've seen him."

"And if he isn't good enough?"

Acker's voice lowered thoughtfully. "I ain't never seen a man could outshoot a scattergun from a dark alley."

Jenney's voice lacked Acker's confidence. "Let's hope

it don't come to that. Now, get out of here. No, use the back way."

Edwin heard the back door open, then close, and the heavy bolt slide in place. Then Jenney's footsteps receded down the hallway, and then all was quiet—quiet, that is, except for the pounding of blood in his ears, and the thumping of his heart so loud he was certain all who passed by on the street out front would hear it.

Lemont stood up from the cot where he'd been cradling his head in his hands when Jenney came through the inner rear door. He wrapped his fingers around the iron bars and said, "Sheriff, I demand to be released! I've broken no laws."

"Obstruction of justice is breaking the law, Mr. Lemont," Jenney said, moving past into the outer office.

"Obstruction—!" Lemont's mouth fell open. "Sheriff, I am innocent; I was forced to involve myself—what little involvement there was! I did not obstruct justice, as you allege. I was merely a witness to the said obstruction!"

Burt Jenney reviewed the ring of keys he'd taken from his desk and selected one. "Lemont," he said putting a key into the lock, "I'm letting you go because I'm tired of listening to your jabbering and trying to make heads or tails out of what it is you're saying." The iron door swung open.

Lemont lowered his eyes at Burt. "Am I to presume I am a free man?" he asked after some deliberation.

"Presume whatever the hell you like, Lemont, only do it somewhere other than my office. Now, get out of here before I change my mind!"

Lemont opened his mouth to protest this rude treat-

ment, but considered the effects of an impertinent remark right at the moment and slowly closed it. He
pulled his hat on his head, squared his shoulders, and
with a great display of wounded dignity turned stiffly
away from the cell and walked out the front door.

24

The breeze, bone-chilling and damp, came off t[he]
mountainside in gusts that stirred the pine trees arou[nd]
the cabin. Even though the rain had stopped falli[ng]
hours ago, fat drops shaken from the heavily lad[en]
boughs swaying overhead continued to pelt the groun[d.]
Beneath the dingy gray sky Dave Thompson saddled h[is]
horse and led the animal from the lean-to shelter.

"See you in a week, Thomas," he said.

Thomas Langely was somber, filled with his ow[n]
thoughts as Dave Thompson swung up into the sadd[le]
and turned the animal onto the steep trail that wou[nd]
out of the mountains and onto the rolling grassland b[e-]
low.

In the quiet morning mist Thomas Langely cou[ld]
hear the stream, swollen with new water, tumble pa[st]
the cabin and down the wooded descent. A bird call[ed]
to its mate, a lonely sound that echoed out of the fog[.]

forest, where chill winds whistled through the weeping pines and hurried angry gray clouds across the skies. He shivered in the lee of the log lean-to and stroked his horse's warm neck. The animal pawed the damp earth, white steam puffing from its nostrils. A trickle of water from the leaky roof filled a muddy pool by the tip of Langely's boot, and all of a sudden he didn't much care for the feeling of being alone. He thought of Sarah Lawrence back in Esteros Creek, and of Dave Thompson on his way home to the Largo—but there was no place for Thomas Langely! He grimaced and started up the muddy path to the cabin. He'd been alone most of his life, why should it start to bother him now?

He poured himself a cup of coffee and tried to master the art of doing nothing. The morning passed slowly as he discovered the location of half a dozen squeaks in the wooden floor. Repeatedly he found his thoughts swimming back to Sarah.

Another log on the fire. He shuffled to the window. The overcast sky depressed him. He thought of the Largo. Its trouble up to now was only the tip of something much bigger, something Burt Jenney was neck deep in. Langely was certain of that. Here, carefully cloistered away from the reach of the law, he was powerless to help!

He'd left Montana with a vow that he'd never again get involved in other folks' problems. Yet it happened just the same. Somehow he had always known that it would. Trouble followed him like a well-trained dog. He dropped into a chair and drummed his fingers on the table, rehashing what he had learned of Esteros Creek. He thought of Jim Kincade and recalled the words the barber had spoken: *It's sort of peculiar, it weren't no com-*

mon bullet, it was one of them new factory-made cartridge bullets.

It was a widespread procedure right after the war to take a cap-and-ball revolver, cut off the back of the cylinder, and bore it out to accept the new metallic cartridge—and both Thaddeus Tyrell and Burt Jenney owned converted pistols. . . .

Langely needed more facts! Marcus Lemont had invited him to dig through his back log of old newspapers, for *interesting kernels of information.* It beat sitting up in the mountains, hiding!

He already felt better as he gulped down the remaining coffee, packed his saddlebags, and carried his gear out to his horse.

Valerie came down the long corridor from her mother's bedroom carrying a dirty breakfast plate and an empty coffee cup. When she entered the kitchen, Sarah looked up from her cup. Valerie set the dishes on the sink.

"How is Martha feeling this morning?"

Valerie frowned. "I'm worried. I've never seen Mother so pale and weak. She's taking it hard. The men, the cattle, and poor old Joe . . ."

"Should I send Dr. Lester by when I get back to town?"

"Mother would be furious if we did that without her consent." Valerie caught a piece of lower lip in her teeth. "But I would feel better if the doctor could take a look at her."

"You tell your mother it was my idea and I couldn't be talked out of it."

"Thank you, Sarah."

"Well, I'd better be going. People will start to wonder why the store is still closed up. Here, let me help you clean these dirty dishes before I leave."

"I'll take care of this. You need to get back to your store."

Sarah wrapped a shawl about her shoulders. On the front porch, where her buggy had been brought around earlier that morning, she looked up at the churning sky and said she hoped it wouldn't start to rain again before she got back. With Valerie's help the two women raised the canvas top and lashed it down.

Valerie said good-bye, and the weary buggy rolled away under the adobe portals and up the road to the rim of the valley. Her long dress whispered over the porch as she turned back to the house, and the day's chores awaited her.

"Where does it hurt?" Dr. Lester asked, his soft finger probing the small of Sidney Lowe's back.

"There . . . oww . . . there," Lowe groaned into the white sheet of the examining table. "Where you poked . . . owww."

"Here?" Lester pressed experimentally with a forefinger.

"Ouch! Yeah, there."

"I don't feel anything." Lester ran a thumb up Lowe's picket-fence spine.

"It hurts something fierce, Doc."

"When did you fall off that horse?"

"This morning."

"Hmmm."

The door to the outer office opened, then closed. Dr. Lester looked up from his patient's naked back and frowned. "I'd best see who that is. I won't be but a minute, Mr. Lowe."

Lowe grunted as Lester left the room, and from the other side of the wall he heard Lester say, "Well, Sarah, whatever can I do for a healthy young girl like you?" Lowe didn't wait to hear her reply. This was the opportunity he had hoped for.

He swung off the table and from his pocket took a slip of paper with the letters of an unpronounceable word carefully penned upon it. At the tall glass-and-wood cabinet against the far wall his eyes swept over the jumble of dark bottles and cardboard boxes with strange labels. He studied each name hurriedly, glancing from the letters written on the slip of paper in his hand and back to the row of bottles, then to the paper and to the bottles again. Up and down the shelves his eyes raced, until they came suddenly to a halt upon one small bottle. Lowe opened the cabinet, snatched it off the shelf, and shoved it into the pocket of his coat, which was lying over the back of a chair. He leaped back to the examining table, still breathing heavily, when a few moments later Dr. Lester returned, shaking his gray head, a frown upon his lips and a wrinkle on his brow.

"Well," Lester said, distracted, "let's see if we can't find what's wrong with your back, young man." He jabbed a finger alongside the raised spine.

"Oww—!"

"Hurt?"

Sidney nodded his head.

"You seem to be doing a lot of sweating," Lester said, probing the moist skin.

Lowe narrowed his eyes at the white sheet.

"Relax, you're all tensed up. I don't feel anything

amiss, but I think you're coming down with a fever. I recommend bed rest for you, young man, and see me again in the morning."

"Thanks Doc, I'll do that."

Valerie had been scrubbing the remains of the morning's breakfast off a plate when a sound from the hallway made her turn sharply. There was the clink of glass touching glass and then a crash as something shattered on the floor. She heard her mother's weak cry. Valerie dropped the washrag and ran down the long hallway to her mother's bedroom.

The crystal pitcher that usually sat on the nightstand lay shattered in a pool of water. A drinking glass had fallen onto its side, dripping water off the wooden table into the pool spreading across the red-tiled floor. Martha Kincade had collapsed half in, half out of the bed, with the tips of her fingers dangled in the water.

"Mother!" Valerie cried. She bolted across the room to the pale figure and gently turned her back onto the bed. Martha's breathing came in raspy, labored pants.

"Mother . . . ?" Valerie grasped the old woman by the shoulders.

Martha's head lolled on the feather pillow, and her lids drew slowly apart, showing very pale liquid-blue eyes.

"Mother . . . what's wrong?"

Martha's vacant stare went past her. Her lips opened and closed in slight, wordless movements. Her once-meaty shoulders felt thin and frail beneath Valerie's hands, as if the muscles there had gone suddenly limp.

Valerie gently shook the old lady. "Mother?"

Martha's caved cheeks seemed to mirror the eyes,

which had sunk deeper into their sockets than Valerie had ever remembered seeing them. She turned them slowly to the girl's frightened face, and a glimmer of recognition flickered in the faintly blue centers. Her lips parted, forming barely audible words. "Jim," she breathed, "Jim . . . where have you been?"

The words were but breath escaping her pale lips. Valerie looked quickly around the room. "It's me, Mother," she cried, tears flowing freely over her high rounded cheeks.

"Yes Jim, I'm ready. . . ."

"Father's not here! Oh, Mother, don't you know me?" Valerie sobbed.

Martha made a great effort to lift her arm and cup a white hand on Valerie's dark forearm. She smiled. "Of course I know you, darling, how could I not—but your father is here now. He wants me to come with him. He beckons to me now from the door." Martha's eyes moved past her again. "You see," she said, "he's wearing his favorite hat, and the new boots we had made for his birthday. Remember? Look, darling, he's behind you."

The tingle of spider's legs crawled up Valerie's spine as she turned, knowing nobody was standing there. "No, Mother, Father is not here," she said. "We'll call the doctor, you're not well."

But Martha seemed not to hear. Her eyes shifted and fixed on the open doorway. A faint smile parted her colorless lips. Then her hand jerked off Valerie's arm and clutched at her shoulder. She twisted violently upon the sheets.

Valerie called for Manuel. The boy appeared in the bedroom door. "Manuel, hurry, get Dave. Mother is sick!" Her desperation spurred the boy quickly out of the house.

Martha's body slackened, her eyes closed, her lips ceased moving, and her breathing became too shallow to detect. Valerie buried her head in the pillow by her mother's shoulder, crying uncontrollably until Dave Thompson's strong hands pulled her away. Bill Tremely helped her from the room.

She resisted at first then conceded to be led away. Bill sat her in a chair at the kitchen table and placed a hand on her trembling shoulder.

A few minutes later a door closed, and Dave's heavy footsteps sounded down the hallway. He came through the kitchen door looking grim. Valerie wiped the tears from her eyes.

"Mother . . . is . . . is she . . . ?" She struggled to regain control of her trembling body. "Mother said Father was waiting to take her with him. She said she was ready."

"I'm sorry, Val, there wasn't anything I could do to help." Dave's brown eyes were, as always, harsh, yet his voice was as gentle as his face was severe.

Valerie composed herself and looked from Dave to Bill Tremely, then back to the tall foreman. "What do I do now?" It wasn't so much a question as a plea.

Through the parlor, beyond the large bay window, some of the ranch hands were gathering on the porch. They seemed to know something was terribly wrong. Valerie said, "Billy, better go out and tell them."

"Yes, ma'am."

Dave Thompson said, "We'll need to be going into town. . . ."

"Strathmore's?" She found she could say the word with no emotion in her voice.

Dave said, "I'll drive you in this afternoon. We'll let the men take your ma in this morning."

Valerie nodded her head slowly. And then they came at her again. She fought them off, knowing she ought to be strong, as her mother had always been, but she couldn't now, and the tears flooded back.

The sun did battle with the clouds, and by noon high blue patches peeked between the tattered gray fringes fleeing across the brightening sky. Langely saddled his horse and checked the Elgin in his vest pocket. Twelve twenty. He climbed into the saddle, turned away from the cabin and started down the mountain trail to the flat land below.

He didn't know exactly where he was when he reached the tall grass, but reckoned it was north of the Porter River, and swung south expecting to find the river and follow it back to the road.

An hour brought him to the rim of a deep chasm— the reservoir created by Jim Kincade's dam, and emptied by Hank Acker's dynamite. It had held water to within a dozen feet from the rim. Now alkali deposits made a ruler-straight line around the canyon wall. The canyon was void of all life—as he imagined the moon might look—except for a slimy green growth that clung to the rock in places, drying and withering in the sun. He turned away and started east along the rim.

The ridge dipped into a long valley where what remained of the Largo herd grazed. He cut through the scattered animals and moved to the edge of the swollen river, wider and swifter now than when he had first seen it. He crossed over to the south bank and followed the waterway until the sight of dead animals, and the swarming flies, forced him up to the top of the ridge to continue at a distance from the trail of death scattered below him.

He arrived at the cottonwood forest in the shank of the afternoon. Stifling heat and humidity from last night's rain still had hold of the land. The road was deserted. Just the same, heeding a warning voice, Langely moved a few hundred yards to one side of it and paralleled it into town.

He reined to a halt on the rise overlooking Esteros Creek as daylight faded against a darkening western horizon. But for a few men on horseback and a half-dozen horses tied up by the Silver Lady Saloon, the streets were empty. A light burned at the rear of the general store. Across the street a match flared behind the windows of the newspaper office followed by the warm yellow glow of lamplight. That told Langely that Lemont was no longer a prisoner in Jenney's jail. He climbed off his horse to wait for the full cover of darkness.

25

The broken-mirror surface of the Rio Gallianas swirled slowly past the sleeping town of Esteros Creek and the crouched figure among the chaparral that thickened along its west bank. In the shadows of the thorny shrubs Hank Acker waited until the sun was long gone, then he quietly slipped away, followed the river a hundred yards, and turned left to sprint across a weedy lot at the rear of the jailhouse.

His quick eyes dug cautiously at the dark alley and into the dim places as he hurried to the heavy wooden door and rapped lightly. Across the alley a shadow passed through the edge of light that stabbed out into the darkness from the rear of the general store. Acker rapped again, more urgently now as the scuffing of a heavy crate being shoved over Sarah's wooden floor disturbed the gentle murmur of the river. The scraping stopped. Acker pounded harder, but not so hard that

Sarah Lawrence might decide to poke her head outside to investigate.

A latch clattered, a bolt slid out, and the door opened. Acker stepped quickly inside. "What took so long?"

Jenney let the question go unanswered, closed the heavy door, and bolted it again. "I thought Lowe was coming with you?"

"In a little while. He's keeping an eye on the newspaper building. Told him to give us enough time to get our nosy desk clerk here ready for his stroll. He'll be around in a few minutes to give us a hand."

"Us!" Burt's eyebrows came together. "I don't know a thing about this until someone comes and tells me the *Esteros Creek Gazette* building is on fire, understand?"

"I understand. Wouldn't want to dirty up your lily-white reputation none, Sheriff."

Jenney swung a contemptuous eye on the younger man, but Acker knew the sheriff still needed his help, at least for the next few hours. Jenney said, "How do you intend to get him over to Lemont's without drawing attention?"

Acker's lips thinned and gave way to a smile. "Walk him," he said. "We'll just walk him like he was too drunk to walk by himself. Between Lowe and me with our hats pulled down so's nobody's likely to recognize us."

"Just like that?"

"Just like that." Acker removed a small bottle from his jacket pocket and casually tossed it in the air and caught it again. "Lowe paid Doc Lester a visit today. When the good doctor wasn't looking, he borrowed this."

"What is it?"

"According to the letters here on the front it is called Clor-ee-form."

"Clor-ee-form . . . ?"

"Uh-huh. It's what doctors use to make people go to sleep. You spill some on a rag, hold it over someone's nose and"—Acker snapped his fingers—"he goes to sleep."

Jenney made a dubious noise in his throat.

"It works sure enough. I seen it with my own eyes when Willard Hanson had that bullet dug out of his hip two years ago—remember?"

Jenney gave Acker a skeptical leer. "We will see. Let's get our pigeon ready."

Edwin fell out of the closet when the door opened, still trussed up, round-eyed fear carved into his smooth face. Jenney untied his ankles and pulled him to his feet. Edwin wobbled and stamped his feet to get the blood moving again.

"Time to take a walk, Edwin," Burt said, removing the gag from the clerk's mouth.

"Where . . . where are you taking me, what are you going to do?" Edwin's tongue licked across the parched scale of his cracked lips.

Acker slipped an old buckskin jacket around Edwin's shoulders and pulled a beat-up hat, two sizes too large, over his eyes. "You don't need to worry about that, you'll sleep through the whole thing."

"Sleep? . . . What do you mean, sleep?"

Jenney pushed Edwin into a chair. Acker came from behind and pressed a damp cloth over his nose and mouth. The sharp odor filled the small hallway, and Edwin struggled against the arms that held him down until his body grew heavy. Slowly his muscles tired, relaxed, and went limp.

"Is he asleep?"

Acker removed the cloth and lifted Edwin's lifeless head. "Like a baby," he said with a grin.

Both men turned at the knock on the front door. Jenney closed the door to the back room, passed through the narrow corridor of iron bars, and closed that door too. In the front office he pulled back a shade for a peek outside, then unlocked the door and let Sidney Lowe in.

"Everything ready?" Lowe asked.

"Come on back." Jenney led him through the long building to the little room at the rear. Lowe looked down at the limp form in the chair. "It worked." He sounded surprised.

"Of course it worked," Acker said. "Come on, let's get him out of here." They hoisted the body between them and followed Burt to the front door. Dressed as he was, Edwin could have been any other drunk that had been bested by John Barleycorn. Jenney poked his head outside, glanced up and down the street, and hurried them out onto the sidewalk.

The trio moved across the muddy street, the one in the center carving two ruts in the spongy road with the tips of his shoes. In a moment the shadows of the Montgomery Hotel swallowed them up.

Langely waited on the ridge above Esteros Creek, chewing thoughtfully on the plug of tobacco he'd bought at Sarah's store that first day. That day seemed so long ago now. The town below darkened as a rising moon spread its chalky light along the valley and danced upon the slow waters of the Rio Gallianas.

When darkness was full upon the land, Langely mounted his horse and rode down into town. He turned up a side street and circled the outlying adobe dwellings, reining to a stop behind the newspaper building in the shadows of a crumbling adobe wall, where broken windows and a gaping, doorless entry peered out like the bleached skulls he'd seen on the cow trails south from Montana.

As he started to dismount, he suddenly halted his motion, then dropped swiftly to the ground and hurried up against the abandoned adobe, pressing into the shadows there. Three men had separated from the darkness at the corner of the newspaper building and had stopped at Lemont's back door. One of the three fell to the ground as if dead . . . or drunk? His bearers didn't seem to care.

They rattled the door handle.

"It's locked!" Langely heard the man with his hand on the door handle say softly. "Go around front and make that old buzzard open this up from the inside. I don't want to have to haul our sleeping friend here in from the street."

Langely crouched into the cover of the tall weeds and worked his way to within a dozen yards of the man standing at the back door. The shadows there masked the man's features, but Langely could see that he was tall and powerfully built. The man bent over the body on the ground to examine the face, then glanced nervously along the back of the building.

A minute passed. Langely heard the man murmur, "Come on, Lowe, what's taking you?"

Another minute. The door swung inward, and a shaft

of light spilled out into the back lot. Lemont's face appeared in the rectangle of the doorway.

"I demand to know the—!" A hand reached from inside and yanked him back. Brandishing a pistol, Lowe stepped quickly outside. "Hurry it up, get him inside!"

They dragged the body into the building, and in the lighted doorway Langely caught a glimpse of a face . . . Hank Acker's face!

Then the door closed. Langely rushed up and flattened himself against the wall. From beyond the door came the sounds of people shuffling about, and Lemont's muffled words demanding to know the meaning of what was going on. The sounds diminished. Langely tried the handle. The door opened, and he slipped inside the back room among a dark disarray of old newspapers, scattered furniture, and boxes piled to the ceiling. A light from the open door to the adjoining room guided him carefully around the clutter that stood indistinctly about.

"What's wrong with this man?" Lemont was demanding.

"He's asleep."

"Asleep?" Lemont gasped. "Why, it's Edwin! Here, sit him down in this chair. I don't understand this."

"Shut up, old man, and sit down."

"I know you," Lemont said, and Langely heard the newspaperman's voice harden. "You're Hank Acker. You killed Joe Lascoe."

"I said shut up!" A sharp crack, and the creak of a chair as someone fell heavily into it. "Draw those shades!"

Langely looked cautiously around the doorway. Lemont was in his chair, his back toward him. Acker had a revolver aimed at him while Lowe, at the window, pulled the shades. Edwin had been propped in a chair in front of Lemont's desk, his head rolled back.

Lemont swiveled to face the two men and leaned slightly forward with his fingers digging into the armrest of his chair. "I demand to know what's going on here."

"You make lots of demands, Lemont," Acker said, "I'm getting tired of hearing them. Word is, you've been talking to that Langely fellow."

"Thomas? We've talked. I don't see what that has to do—"

"The sheriff seems to think he told you certain things and you're about to poke your nose in where it shouldn't be."

Langely heard the frown in Lemont's voice. "Burt Jenney! So that's it. No wonder you're not in jail for Joe's killing. You *did* kill him?"

Acker glanced at Lowe and grinned. "No way we'll ever know which gun the bullet came from, but we were both trying."

Lowe laughed. "We sure were, old man."

Lemont wagged his head. "You're violent men, both of you." He looked at the unconscious desk clerk. "What did you do to poor Edwin?"

"Like we said, he's asleep, just like you're gonna be in a minute." Acker removed the small bottle from his pocket. "Lowe took it from Doc Lester's medicine cabinet. It's something called Clor-ee-form."

"Chloroform!" Lemont exclaimed. "That's a dangerous chemical! You can kill a man with that!"

"Now, wouldn't that be a shame." Acker came around the desk and pulled open the drawers. He found Lemont's pistol in the top drawer and tucked it in his belt. In the bottom drawer he located a bottle of whiskey. "Looky here, Sidney, look what Mr. Lemont has in his desk." He opened the bottle and took a long swallow and handed it to Lowe. "Seems a shame to waste it all."

Lowe took a mouthful. "It sure does seem a waste—but Jenney wants it to look good. Suppose we can get ole Burt to supply us with a fresh bottle when we finish up here?"

"You scoundrels," Lemont said. "You intend to kill us!"

Acker said, "You catch on real quick, Mr. Newspaperman. And after we finish here with you, we're going to plan us an accident for the Lawrence girl and her goody-goody Indian friend."

Langely eased his revolver from the holster, backed into the shadows, and stepped in front of the open doorway.

"You see, Lemont," Acker said while Lowe spilled whiskey over the desk, "you and Edwin here are about to drink yourselves insensible—or at least that's the way it will appear. No one will ever know for sure seeing as both of you will be killed in the fire that started when you 'accidentally' knocked over a lamp." As Acker spoke, he poured the chloroform onto a cloth. "You see, people get careless when they drink too much—"

"I don't think so, not tonight," Langely said from the darkness of the adjoining room. His words riveted the men, and the whiskey bottle slipped from Lowe's fingers. Langely stepped into the light and shot a quick glance at Sidney Lowe. "Try for it."

Lowe's hand stopped and carefully backed away from the revolver on his hip.

"Thank God!" Lemont exclaimed.

Langely motioned with his revolver. "You boys stand over there, away from the desk. Marc, relieve your visitors of their hardware."

"With pleasure," Lemont said, standing.

At once Langely realized his error. He read it instantly in Lowe's eyes, and in that brief moment when Lemont's body moved between them, Lowe's gun appeared in his hand and fired.

The bullet tugged at Langely's sleeve. He dove behind Lemont's heavy desk as a second shot exploded overhead. Lemont stumbled backward, knocking the lamp over. Coal oil poured across the floor, pulling a sheet of blue fire after it. Acker and Lowe leaped for the front door. Langely rolled from behind the desk and fired. Acker stumbled, caught himself on the door frame, and then he was gone.

Langely scrambled to his feet and pulled Lemont from the fire, beating the flames off the old man's clothing. Marcus rolled to his back with a crimson stain spreading across his white shirt above his belt.

Langely flung a bright Mexican blanket off the back of the settee and whipped at the flames that had started up the shades. He ripped them down and threw them out the door. Men came in from the street to help stamp out the last of the blaze.

Langely heaved a box of lead typeface through the glass window and fanned at the thick black smoke, then he knelt by Lemont's side. Lemont's eyes parted and looked up. "Get him?"

"I wounded one, I think. I'm sorry Marc—"

Lemont coughed, "It was my own stupid fault for crossing between you two."

Langely called for someone to get the doctor.

Lemont grimaced and shook his head. "Don't bother," and he waved a finger at his desk. "I found that paper, the one you suggested I should look up. I didn't know what to make of your cryptic references to Burt's gun the other night. In fact I had to read the article twice before I made the connection." He coughed, and a trickle of blood creased the corner of his mouth and down his trembling chin.

"Not a bad piece of journalism, I might add," Lemont continued, his chest heaving with each painful breath. "It took me a while, then all of a sudden two and two added up to four, and I realized where we had all gone wrong. We all assumed that Thaddeus Tyrell killed Jim Kincade because of their recent trouble and because Tyrell happened to have a gun that matched the bullet. Now it seems Burt Jenney possesses the same kind of gun, and he came on the scene only moments afterward —enough time to shoot Kincade in the back from the side door while Jim was facing Tyrell. His shot must have started them all to shooting, and Jenney let them play it out until there weren't enough men left alive to verify Tyrell's story. In the confusion who could be sure anyway. Then the smoke clears, all but two are dead, and enters the sheriff, Burt Jenney, a man with an ax to grind and one who is above suspicion."

"Don't talk, Marc."

Lemont coughed. His face twisted, and he drew his knees up as if a stab of pain had shot through his belly. "Don't stop me now," he said. "It's the last chance I'll ever have. Thomas, in my pocket—the flask—I sure could use a drink."

Langely dug the silver flask out of Lemont's breast

pocket, but Lemont was already gone by time he put it to the old man's lips.

Slowly, he closed the flask and stood. With sudden determination he pushed through the crowd at the door. Someone said Lowe and Acker had run into the saloon.

Langely studied the dark street, ignoring their stares and the burning sting of his arm as he stepped down and strode toward the saloon.

26

A checkered-vest gent with slick-flat hair parted down the middle craned his neck over his shoulder and banged out a parade of sour notes on the piano.

Talk trailed off as heads turned. Eyes glanced out of dark corners. Faces looked out of beer mugs. Langely stopped inside the batwing doors and viewed the long, smoky room in a single glance. At the rear of the saloon beaded curtains hid the entrances to more private alcoves. The bar to his right was a heavy abutment running nearly from front to back of the building. Behind the bar's polished brass rails a long mirror reflected ranks of glasses, legions of assorted bottles, and the confusion of tables and patrons beyond; wide hats, small-brim bowlers, and no hats at all. In the reflection the Silver Lady Saloon appeared twice as wide. Overhead, chandeliers made black spots on the ceiling.

Langely glanced back at the man having trouble

keeping the piano on tune. The musician's head had developed a nervous jerk, turning from the instrument to the batwings and back again, and all the while he missed notes and seemed to be doing a lot of perspiring. It was not overly warm inside the saloon, though Langely's own forehead had begun to sweat.

At the tip of his boot a still-moist spot stained the wooden floor a bright crimson. He shifted his eyes, saw another splash angling left, and a third, closer to the wall.

Slowly the normal saloon noises resumed. Langely stepped up to the bar and watched the crowded floor at his back in the long mirror. The bartender came by. Langely said, "Two men just came in here."

"I seen lots o' men, mister, both coming and going. I don't pay no mind to nothin' but pouring drinks."

"You would have paid attention to these two. One of 'em was bleeding like a stuck pig from a bullet I put in him."

The bartender's fat, pink hand slipped off the bar as he glanced at Langely's arm. "And someone did the same to you, it would appear," he said. "I told you, mister, I don't pay no attention to—"

Langely's revolver appeared and leveled at the fat man's chin, cutting off his patter. "Bring it out, real slow and careful."

The other's eyes grew dark. He placed the sawed-off shotgun on the polished bar. "Mister, you're asking for trouble. Those fellows have friends in here."

Langely pulled the shotgun near and cracked the action to check the chambers. "I'll ask you again. Where are they?"

The bartender's thick lips tightened. Langely glanced

beyond him at the mirror and saw that the piano player was sitting on the very edge of his stool, beating the ivories with little regard now for the noise he was making. Watching the musician's reflection, Langely's grin came back at him and he said, "Hank Acker. You have just ten seconds to step out. After that I start shooting up the place!"

Chairs scuffed back, men diving out of them. A shadow moved on the wall behind the tired old piano, and Langely swung the shotgun around. The musician yelped and tumbled backward off his stool. Both barrels went off almost simultaneously.

Acker stumbled out from behind the piano. His revolver fired into the wooden floor, his face went wide with shock, and he looked down at himself as if unable to believe the holes leaking blood onto his fingers. He staggered a step backward against the wall, hung there a moment, then made a bloody smear to the floor. Men started for the doors, while the tortured wires within the shattered piano sang a slow-dying wail.

Langely cracked the shotgun, ejected the spent hulls, and held his hand out. The fat man blinked and closed his mouth. He reached into his dirty apron for two more shells. Langely fed them into the scattergun, closed the breech, and swung it around, burying its short barrel into the barkeeper's fleshy belly.

"There was a second man." Langely's eyes narrowed.

"Out back—he went out the back door," the fat man stammered.

Faces gawked from behind tables and at the far ends of the bar, but they gave him a wide field as he headed toward the rear of the saloon.

* * *

Sarah Lawrence paused on the sidewalk and looked at the dark doors of Strathmore's Undertaking Parlor. It was not a place she enjoyed visiting, especially in the gloom that followed sunset, but she knew she was stalling. It was so hard to know what to say at a time like this. She glanced at the faintly illuminated windows and turned the brass doorknob.

Valerie Kincade was sitting in a chair, alone, when Sarah stepped inside. She looked up with swollen eyes.

"Val, I'm so sorry," she said, going to her friend.

Valerie glanced down at the handkerchief, bunched and knotted in her fingers, and said, "Dave is in the back making the arrangements."

"Is there anything I can do?"

At that moment Dave Thompson came through the doorway with a solemn face, Artemus Strathmore leading the way. Strathmore was an austere man in a black coat. The undertaker peered over the rim of his spectacles at Valerie and began to say something consoling, when the sound of gunfire outside interrupted him.

Two shots rang out, close together, followed by a third a moment later. When the street quieted down, Artemus Strathmore cleared his throat and resumed his consolatory words.

Sarah went to the windows and parted the curtains. "There's trouble at the newspaper building," she said, reaching for the door. Valerie remained seated as Dave followed Sarah out the door. Strathmore frowned at the second interruption.

Up the street smoke poured from the windows of the newspaper building. Dave glanced at the crowd gathering on the sidewalk in front of Lemont's office and stepped back inside to retrieve his hat. "There's a fire at the newspaper building, Val," he said. "They're going to need help putting it out."

Valerie nodded her head. Artemus Strathmore directed a baleful eye at her and apologized for the untimely interruption. His mournful voice was that of a man who spent his life consoling the bereaved, and it made Sarah itch.

Dave hurried up the street and through the crowd. Inside the smoky building Dr. Lester was directing two men to help with Lemont's body. "What happened?"

Lester shook his head. "Poor Marcus, killed by thugs."

"Who did it?"

Someone in the crowd said, "It was Hank Acker and Sidney Lowe."

Someone else said, "That stranger, the gunfighter, he went after 'em."

"Thomas? But he—" Dave stopped. That Langely didn't intend spending a full week in hiding, Dave had suspected, but he hadn't expected him to show up so soon. "Where did he go?"

"They went into the—"

The roar of a double-barrel shotgun brought their heads around.

". . . saloon," the man finished.

Dave hurried across the street and burst through the batwings as Hank Acker's body was being dragged away from the shattered piano. The bartender had a bottle of whiskey turned up in his shaking hands, gulping the amber fluid down like it was water. Langely wasn't there. The men peering out the back door told Dave the direction he had gone.

* * *

High weeds brushed his thighs as he slid along the dark adobe wall of the La Casa Luna where the light of the large moon could not quite reach him. The field behind was gray beneath the night sky, and beyond glinted the slow waters of the Gallianas River. He halted at the edge of the wall to study the dark trees behind the jail. His hand squeezed the shotgun and relaxed, squeezed and relaxed in slow, rhythmic waves that drained the tension from him as he searched the shadowed landscape of dark buildings.

From somewhere out in the dark came a metallic click. Langely leaped to the ground even as the harsh report of a pistol shattered the stillness of the night air. A chunk of adobe mud exploded from the wall behind him. Langely sighted the muzzle flash and sprang to his feet, diving for the cover of empty wooden shipping crates piled high against the back of Sarah's store.

The stillness returned to the night. He lay in the comforting embrace of the darkness, counting slowly to twenty, then in a single rush advanced to a position that afforded a view down the alleyway. It was empty now, and he hurried along the dark passageway.

Except for the gathering crowd around Lemont's office, the main street was strangely deserted when he stepped out onto it. Beneath the shadows of the Montgomery Hotel a movement caught his eye. Side by side came the flash and the bark of a pistol, and a bullet tore through the fleshy part of his calf. Langely dropped to the roadway, rolling behind a watering trough. Two more shots rang out.

He fumbled a dirty bandanna from his pocket and tied it around his leg above the wound. In a minute his leg would be afire, but for now a tingling numbness held back the torment. Hitching himself up on one elbow, he peered around the trough. A shadow moved among the shadows. Langely swung the shotgun around and squeezed both triggers.

27

The two blasts sounded as one, followed by the squall of splintering wood where the double head of buckshot ripped out a corner of the wall a dozen inches from his head.

Sidney Lowe flung himself back against the clapboard siding, and when the night grew quiet again, peeked around the corner of the building and down the long, empty street. Sticky sweat trickled over the bridge of his nose and ran warm and salty into his mouth. He could only guess where Langely had disappeared to, or where he would turn up next. Fighting for control over his trembling fingers, he replaced the spent cartridges in his revolver and hurried down the side street toward the alley at the rear of the Montgomery Hotel.

Langely hobbled up against a cool, dark wall and leaned the empty shotgun there. The wound in his leg had become a fierce pain, as if a hot iron had been shoved through his flesh. His pant leg grew heavy with blood, and the swelling torment more than erased the sting in his arm where back in Lemont's office Lowe's bullet had but creased the skin.

He paused against a wall, breathing ragged as if he'd dog-jogged a mile, and allowed his head to clear as he sleeved his brow and tried to put the pain out of mind. Then he limped toward the rear of the Montgomery Hotel, halting at the corner for a wary glance around it. In the pale light that shown at the far end, Sidney Lowe, equally cautious, stepped out and looked around. He peered down the alley without seeing Langely and then turned to study the other side of the street.

Langely pushed himself away from the building and called out, "Lowe!"

Lowe spun around. His gun came up, and the two shots echoed down the back-street canyon.

And then the night was still again.

Sweat poured down Langely's neck. His head began to spin, and he had to brace himself against the hotel. As he started down the alley, he was vaguely aware of a warm wetness sloshing in his boot. . . .

The ground lurched under his feet.

He shot out a hand, caught himself against the hotel wall. Drawing in deep breaths no longer worked to clear his head as pushed himself up straight again. He hobbled along the back side of the hotel and out into the street where Lowe was sprawled in the mud of yesterday's rain.

Lowe's fingers dug spasmodically a moment at the clay beneath his face, then ceased moving. When

Langely bent and turned him over, his eyes opened slowly.

"Where's Burt Jenney?"

Blood choked the words in Lowe's throat, and his body shuddered. Then his eyes rolled up in his head one last time, and Langely eased the body back to the mud.

"Looking for me?"

Langely stiffened.

"Drop the gun," Jenney said from behind him.

Langely stood and turned. The sheriff came across the street with a Winchester under his right hand, his left wrapped around the waist of Sarah Lawrence. He stopped. A dozen feet—and the struggling woman—separated them.

"I said drop it, Langely!"

Sarah said, "I'm sorry, Thomas. I heard the shooting, and then someone said you were in town. I went to look and . . ." She turned her face up at Jenney.

Langely dropped his revolver. He didn't think much of a man who would hide behind a woman's skirt, but then his opinion of Burt Jenney had been on a steady decline anyway. He said, "Acker and Lowe are both dead. How many more do you have on your payroll, Jenney?"

Jenney glanced down at the body lying in the street. "He was so cocksure he could take you. I'm real pleased to see that you let the wind out of his bag, Langely. Saved me the trouble."

"Trouble, Sheriff?" Thomas Langely found a laugh somewhere within him. "Your troubles are just beginning. Lowe and Acker spilled the whole story to Lemont before they shot him. Before Marc died, he confirmed my suspicions about you and Jim Kincade—and with plenty of men around to hear it." A wave of dizziness swept to over him. He staggered, and when it passed, he said, "I've learned a lot about Esteros Creek's history in the short time I've been here."

Sarah stopped struggling, suddenly curious.

"It seems it displeased you some when the Kincades adopted Valerie. That cut you out of any share you may have gotten in the Largo."

"It displeased me some," Jenney agreed.

"It displeased you enough to shoot Jim Kincade in the back! It was only fortunate that the circumstances were as they were—Jim and Thaddeus Tyrell together with a bunch of gun-toting ranch hands to back them. Fortunate, too, that Thaddeus Tyrell happened to be carrying a newly converted revolver similar to yours—"

Jenney laughed. "Fortune had nothing to do with it. I planned it that way." His face darkened. "I had a rightful claim to the Largo. I stuck by Jim Kincade like he was kin—like the son he never had! *I* deserved part share in the Largo, not some squaw!"

Langely glanced past the sheriff's shoulder, his eyes suddenly drawn to movement there. Dave Thompson step out from between two buildings. Langely shifted his view back to Jenney. "Your plan almost worked too. The Largo was within your reach." He felt the ground move beneath him and struggled to hold on to consciousness. His talk was becoming disjointed, yet he had to keep it up, had to keep Jenney's attention while Dave eased into position. "Too bad folks heard what Lemont had to say before he died—"

Sarah started squirming again. Jenney tightened his grip.

"You're finished in this town," Langely said, raising

his voice as Dave Thompson came up behind Jenney. "You can forget the Largo. Your problem will be getting out of Esteros Creek now that everyone knows the truth."

A sneer twisted Burt's lips. "That may be *my* problem, Langely, but I'm still the law here, and folks think twice before confronting the law—respectable folks, that is. Respectable people keep out of other people's business, as you should have." His fingers tightened on the Winchester. "At least I still *have* my problems. In a few seconds yours will be all over—or just beginning, depending on how you believe. Since you were the one that opened up this can o' worms, it's only fitting you be buried with it." Jenney tilted up the Winchester.

Dave Thompson yelled, "Jenney!"

Burt swung around and fired. Dave's arms flung wide. Langely leaped for his gun as Sarah's teeth sunk into the back of Burt's hand.

Jenney yelped and cast the girl aside, levering a shell into the rifle. Langely grabbed his pistol up out of the mud as he rolled and brought it around. In a glimpse he saw Sarah tumbled away, and the rifle coming back around.

Langely fired.

The .45 took Jenney full in the stomach.

The sheriff buckled, and in a death spasm his trigger finger tightened on the trigger and the rifle went off.

Something hit Langely's hip. It hit bone. It hit hard and kicked him back to the ground. He forgot the throbbing in his calf as a greater pain drew a gray blanket over him. He was vaguely aware that his hip felt disjointed, as if a portion if it had been moved to a different part of his body—then he saw Sarah. She hovered over him indistinctly, through a fog growing thick in front of his eyes. He tried to move and couldn't. He imagined he heard his name being called. Sarah's lips moved, but he couldn't hear the words—the fog swirled in. The night grew darker, and Sarah's face faded with the light.

He sensed that people were gathering around him. Someone touched him, he felt their hands distantly, as though he were detached and watching from afar. Then his body was lifted from the ground and a razor-sharp pain shot through his skull, driving consciousness away.

28

Sarah hauled back on the reins and brought the little buggy to a halt atop the ridge. "Well, there it is."

A wisp of gray smoke curled from the house in the valley below. With the October chill in the air, the house was a friendly sight, but Thomas Langely knew a twinge of loneliness in the vacant outbuildings, the empty corrals, and deserted grounds. The Largo was only a name now, a remembrance of something that had once been great.

"How is Valerie doing?"

"Val is doing just fine. After all, she's a Kincade."

He grinned. "That she is."

Sarah shivered in the wind that whipped along the ridge top. "We'd better be getting on down there. I don't want our sightseeing to hold up dinner." She raised the reins, then hesitated and looked at him. "Would you care to drive the rest of the way in?"

He waved away the offered straps. "You're doing just fine. Besides, Lester said I could come only if I promised to take it easy. I wouldn't want him to lose faith in his star patient."

Sarah smiled at him and snapped the reins. The buggy clattered off the ridge, drawn easily along the dusty road by the single horse. Langely was enjoying the ride, his first opportunity to get away from Esteros Creek and out from under Lester's eagle eye in over two months. During those months while he lay in bed, at first teetering between life and death, the summer had slipped away, and now the coolness of fall had arrived. The October chill was a welcome change for the northerner.

Tall, brittle grass moved with the breeze, and as the buggy rumbled down to the house, coveys of quail darted haphazardly in front of the horse. He was seeing the countryside differently, now that the trouble was over.

The trial that had sent Martin Caldwell to the territorial prison in Santa Fe had finally brought to light the truth about Big Jim Kincade's death. Once the facts were known, the tensions between the Largo and the Double T had eased, but it all came too late.

He looked over at Sarah's glowing cheeks, the small gray puffs of her breath, her gloved hands holding the reins between their fingers as she expertly guided the buggy down the narrow road. It had been two months now since he'd put up his gun for good, and no longer did that naked feeling haunt him like it had the first time. He felt at peace now. It was a good feeling, a feeling he hoped would last a long time.

The buggy clattered under the adobe portals, into the

courtyard. Sarah brought it to a stop alongside a long carriage, where two men, bundled against the chill, talked with Valerie. They stopped when Sarah pulled up.

The driver of the carriage, buttoned into a heavy coat with a hat pulled down on his head, was a young man. His passenger was considerably older and clutched a cane in his gloved hand, a cane much like the one Langely used now.

Sarah said, "Mr. Tyrell, Jeff, it's good to see you again."

The old man nodded his head.

Valerie was standing on the porch with a shawl bundled about her shoulders and her long black hair hanging loose at her waist. She said, "Mr. Tyrell, this is Mr. Langely."

The old man looked across to him. "So, you're the bee that got into this town's bonnet," he said. "I should be mad as hell at you! I lost a lot of good men in the housecleaning after the trial." His stern face cracked with a smile. "But I'm not. I'm glad you came along to get the whole sticky mess finally cleaned up. Hope you'll be staying a while. Come on out to the ranch someday."

"I just may take you up on that, Mr. Tyrell. I've heard a lot about you."

The old man winked. "Don't believe a word of it."

Langely at once liked the old man.

Thaddeus Tyrell said, "We were just about to leave." He tipped his hat to Sarah, and to Langely said, "Be seeing you sometime." Tyrell glanced back at Valerie. "Keep my offer in mind, Miss Kincade."

"I will."

Jeff Tyrell turned the team away, and the carriage rolled out onto the south road.

Valerie said, "Well, come on down from there and get inside." She glanced to the gray skies. "Looks like an early winter this year." She shivered beneath the shawl.

Sarah climbed out of the buggy and came around the other side. Langely waved her away. "Folks been helping me in and out of things for the last two months. I want to do it myself now."

Sarah stood back, folded her arms, and frowned. "But if you fall . . ."

"If I fall, you have my permission to pick me up." He swung his leg stiffly over the side and eased himself to the ground. His back ached as if he'd slept with a rock under his bedroll, and he groaned as he straightened up. "Two weeks ago I couldn't walk without help. Now I'm climbing in and out of buggies all by myself. Quite an improvement, wouldn't you say?"

Sarah laughed. She wrapped an arm around his waist and helped him up the steps to the porch.

"You're looking much better, Thomas," Valerie said, holding the door for him.

He stopped and regarded the lovely Indian woman. "And you're looking well, too, Valerie." He nodded at the empty compound and deserted, boarded-up windows. "All the men leave?"

"All but Billy and Edgar. They're staying on while I tie up the loose ends, but I know they're itching to move on too. There is nothing left here for them."

Langely shook his head, feeling the loneliness of vacant buildings.

Sarah shivered. "It's cold out here. I hope you have a pot of hot tea on, Val."

The house was warm. Sarah moved a chair in front of the stone fireplace and helped him into it. Then she leaned over and said, "Now, will you be all right for a few minutes, darling, while I help Val?"

"I think I can manage," he said, hooking his walking stick over the arm of the chair.

She kissed his forehead and left to help Valerie with the tea. He relaxed in the overstuffed chair and looked around the vast room. It had a feeling of permanence about it. A welcomed feeling to a man who had known little more than hotel rooms and the open sky. Sitting in that big chair, with the fire at his feet, and Sarah in the next room, he was content. All that was required to make life perfect was a big, friendly dog curled on the hearth rug—a dog that could work quail, he mused, recalling the coveys that had flushed across the road on the ride out. If only he were able to walk more than a half-dozen steps at a time! There was always next year. Lester had assured him that by spring he'd be walking nearly normally. When fall rolled around, he'd be back with a shotgun and that bird dog, he promised himself.

The women returned with tea and spice cake, and after a moment Sarah said, "Darling, Val told me she was leaving the Largo. She's moving back east."

It wasn't news that surprised him. "Is that true?"

She nodded her head. "I can't run the place, Thomas, my heart isn't in it now that Mother and Dave are gone. Besides, there is nothing left to run, and I have no one in Esteros Creek who will miss me but you and Sarah."

"Val has a gentleman friend in New York!" Sarah said.

"I hope everything works out for you. When are you leaving?"

"Oh, not until after the wedding. I wouldn't miss that for the world. Then of course I have the affairs of the ranch to take care of. I need to find a buyer. . . ." She paused. "Mr. Tyrell has offered to buy the place, but I wouldn't feel right selling it to him, knowing the way Mother felt. Of course that was before we knew the truth about Father's death. Still, it just wouldn't seem right." Valerie hesitated. "You wouldn't know of anyone who would be interested in buying the Largo, would you, Thomas?"

He grinned. "I don't know anyone with the kind of money it would take to buy this place." He glanced at Sarah, and she was wrestling with a smile.

Valerie shrugged her shoulders, a glimmer of mischief flickering in her black eyes. "Well, you know we only have a few hundred head of cattle left, and they are scattered throughout the hills. Likely most will never be found again. Then there's that leaky barn, not worth much as it stands. The corrals need fence-mending, and —well, I guess what I am trying to say is that I wouldn't feel right asking a whole lot of money for the place, and of course I wouldn't need it all at once. I'd want a few thousand to clear up the loans at the bank, then perhaps another two thousand to see me on my way. . . . I wouldn't expect to be paid in full until the Largo is back on its feet making money, and then the new owners could send me part of the balance every year. I'd work out terms."

Sarah was laughing now. Langely frowned.

"Darling," Sarah said, "Valerie is offering *us* the ranch."

"Consider it my wedding present to you two," Val added quickly.

He shifted his eyes between the two women. They were enjoying his shock. He didn't speak for a moment, and when he did, he pointed out that they didn't even have the few thousand dollars Valerie needed to clear up the loans.

"Mr. Easterman has been trying to buy the store ever since Dad died. If I sold it, we'd have more than enough money to put down on the Largo, and maybe some left over to start building up the herd again."

Valerie said, "The ranch is mine to sell anyway I like to whomever I like . . . and I'd like to sell it to you." She waited for his answer.

He looked around the grandiose house—almost too big as far as houses went. It was a sturdy place, a place to put down roots and raise a family. He'd always wanted kids.

He felt the past releasing its hold on him, slipping away like an old garment ready for the rag bag, and it was a good feeling. He looked into Sarah's eager face and sparkling-blue eyes. *Why not!* He turned back to Valerie with a grin as wide as all of New Mexico on his face.

"I don't suppose you would have a good bird dog to throw into the deal?"